DIARY OF A BLACK COCK HUNGRY
WHITE SISSY

THE COMPLETE STORY

BY
MARCI WILCOX

ISBN-13: 978-0-9986272-2-9

CHAPTER ONE
THE SEARCH FOR RAEGAN

I'd never been to this part of town before. To be honest, I'd never had the nerve. Whenever the local news did a story about drugs, shootings, or desperate poverty, it always took place in this neighborhood. The houses were falling apart, the yards were choked with weeds, and dirty children played in the street.

I drove slowly and kept checking the address I'd scrawled on a sheet of paper. The house had to be on this street. People stopped what they were doing to stare at me. I'm sure they were wondering what a white man in a Lexus was doing driving down their street.

What was I doing here? Why was I searching for a wife who left me without saying where she was going or why she was leaving? I thought Raegan and I had the perfect marriage, but then without warning she quit her job, packed a few of her belongings in a single suitcase, and said goodbye.

For weeks, I moped around the house trying to make sense of what happened. When the divorce papers arrived, I refused to sign them. If she wanted a divorce, she'd have to face me and give me an explanation for why she broke my heart.

Finally, it dawned on me to question my next-door neighbor, Emily Ann. She and Raegan had been close, but had a falling out shortly before Raegan left. I had been too depressed to see that there might be a connection.

Emily Ann was all too happy to talk, but the story she told was too incredible to be true. The woman Emily Ann described couldn't possibly be my Raegan. My wife would never do the disgusting things that Emily Ann claimed she'd done.

"She's into black guys now," Emily Ann said. "And not just one at a time. She's a black cock hungry white slut."

Her words were like bullets shooting out of her mouth at me.

"I don't believe you," I said. "That doesn't sound like Raegan at all."

"The sooner you accept the truth; the sooner you'll get over her."

"I don't care what she's done. I need to find her."

"She started hanging out with the father of one of the students she was advising. His name started with a Q. That's all I know."

I went to Golden Heights Predatory Academy to see if they could help me locate this Q person. They were still upset that Raegan had quit so abruptly and refused to talk to me. Dejected, I got in my car and was about to drive away when a huge black man in a janitor's uniform tapped on my window.

"You Miz Blankenship's husband?" he said.

"Yes. Do you know where she is?"

"Maybe I do. Maybe I don't."

I took out my wallet and gave him what I had on me. He counted the bills before stuffing them in the pocket of his stained coveralls.

"She living with Quintavius. He don't treat her right. Woman like Miz Blankenship deserve better than that ghetto trash."

He gave me Quintavius' full name and address. I scribbled it down on a sheet of paper.

"Thank you," I said. "I never did get your name."

"Tyrone."

"Thank you, Tyrone."

"I wouldn't be too quick to thank me."

"It's okay. I don't mind paying for the information."

"It's not that. See, I done fucked her a few times too."

I was too shocked to say anything. I put the car in gear and drove away.

The house number was on the battered mailbox. In the front yard a dirty swing set sat in a patch of mud. A dented Escalade was parked in the gravel driveway. I got out of the car and looked around nervously, expecting a gun shot at any moment. I resisted the urge to dash to the house.

I reminded myself that I was here to get my beloved wife. With determination, I strode to the house and knocked on the front door. I could hear rap music blasting inside. Figuring that whoever was inside hadn't heard me; I banged on the door.

The music died. The curtains over the front window fluttered briefly and I caught a quick glimpse of someone peering out at me. The door flew open and I found myself staring down the barrel of a big, shiny handgun.

"Who the fuck are you?" growled the owner of the gun.

"I'm Raegan's husband. I demand that you let me see her."

The hammer clicked. The metallic sound made my knees weak and I felt a warm spot on my crotch. I'd peed in my pants, but thankfully just a little and not enough to send a warm yellow stream down my leg.

"You demand?"

I gathered up my courage. If I was going to die here on this doorstep, then I wasn't going to die as a coward.

"Yes. I'm still her husband. I have a right to see her. Is she inside?"

"Get your ass inside before the neighbors start to talk."

He lowered the gun and moved inside. I followed him to a dingy living room. Take-out cartons and empty beer cans were everywhere. Despite the mess, there was an empty feeling in the house. I knew that feeling intimately because I was living with it too. Raegan wasn't here. Nobody was here. He was alone.

We sat on opposite sides of the room. He wore a pair of baggy boxer shorts and nothing else. I could see the outline of his dick, which made me think about Emily Ann's claim that Raegan had become...how did she put it? A black cock hungry white slut.

He didn't need to whip out his cock for me to know that he was well-endowed. Its massive size made me feel self conscious about the size of my own cock. I had a good size cock and no woman had ever had reason to complain, but these black men's monster cocks were intimidating. However, the gun he held loosely in his lap was even more intimidating.

"Are you Quintavius?"

He eyed me suspiciously.

"How you know that?"

"I heard Raegan was living with you."

He pointed the gun at me.

"Who told you?"

"It doesn't matter. Where's Raegan?"

"It matters to me. Snitches sleep in ditches."

"Raegan told me where to find her in case of an emergency."

I don't know why I lied. I'd paid Tyrone for Quintavius' address. I didn't owe the fat janitor anything.

Quintavius leaped off the couch and pressed the barrel against the side of my head. His eyes were wide with fury. I gripped the armrests of the chair and felt cold sweat run down my back.

"You lying!" he shouted. "Raegan would never have told your white ass where to find her. Not without my permission."

He leaned over me so that I was eye level with his torso. His boxers had drooped down to the point where I could see the base of his cock surrounded by black curly pubic hair. I could even make out the beginning of a large vein in the middle of his cock.

Gripping a gun must have been like holding a dick because his was starting to strain the fabric of his shorts. It was disgusting. The worse part was the smell, like burnt cocoa butter mixed with an old jockstrap. No, the smell wasn't the worse part. Realizing that this man had fucked my wife was the part that made me want to retch. She had preferred his dick to mine. For one horrifying second, an image of his dark naked skin sweating and grunting over Raegan's milky white body as she moaned with pleasure flashed into my mind. I wanted to kill this man. I wanted to rip that gun out of his hand and blow his head right off shoulders or have him kill me so the image of the two of them together would never enter my brain again.

"I just want to talk to my wife," I said. "I can't live without her so if you're not going to tell me where she is, then you might as well blow my fucking brains out right here and now!"

We glared at each other for what felt like an hour but was probably less than a minute. Quintavius let his arm drop to his side and he laughed.

"I ain't going to kill you," he said. "I don't need that kind of trouble and you ain't fucking worth it. But I will let somebody else do the job for me. You really want to know where Raegan is?"

"I believe I've made that abundantly clear."

Quintavius went back to the couch. He dug a cigarette out of a pack on the coffee table and lit it. He took a drag and let the smoke out slowly.

"You ever hear of Rodney Robinson?"

"The basketball player?"

"Yeah."

"He played for the Pacers. He retired like five years ago."

"That's right."

"I get it. Raegan left you for him."

"You would think that, wouldn't you white boy? Truth is, I lost a bet to Rodney and didn't have the money to cover it."

I clenched my fists. I wanted to jump across the room and beat his face in, but I'd never make it before he shot me.

"You gave him Raegan? How could you gamble with somebody else's life?"

Quintavius took another drag on his cigarette.

"Don't judge me. When you don't have money, you pay with whatever you got. Now if you want her back, then you going to have to deal with Mr. Robinson."

For all his bravado, I picked up on the fear in his voice. He was as worried about Raegan as I was. I didn't know what bothered me more. The fact that he and I had something in common: a relationship with Raegan. Or that Raegan was in a situation that would cause a hood rat like him to be concerned about her welfare.

Raegan, what had you gotten yourself into?

CHAPTER TWO
TRADING PLACES

I'd never been to this part of town before. To be honest, I'd always wanted to. Whenever the local news did a story about the rich and famous, it always took place in this neighborhood. The homes were not mere houses. They were elegant mansions with manicured lawns, swimming pools, and expensive cars.

I couldn't see Rodney Robinson's mansion from the road because of the forest of tall trees on his property, which was surrounded by a high iron gate. There was a security guard in a small hut stationed at the entrance. I pulled up to the hut and a beefy guard in an official looking uniform slid open his window.

"Do you have an appointment?" he asked. He held a clipboard in his hand.

"No, I don't. I'm here to see someone who is staying here. Her name is Raegan. She's my wife."

"What's your name?" He looked at his clipboard.

"Cole Blankenship." The guard ran his finger down the list of names. "I'm not going to be on that list. I just came to see..."

"It's right here. Mr. Robinson is expecting you. Drive up to the top of the driveway and park behind the fountain."

He closed his window. The gates slowly opened and I drove inside.

I could think of only one reason why Robinson knew I was coming. Quintavious must have called him. That meant they were closer than I expected. I was never under the illusion that getting Raegan back was going to be easy, but I never imagined that I would have to confront a basketball legend.

The driveway snaked back and forth as I drove higher and higher. Once I broke through the dense trees, there was beautiful green grass punctuated by Dogwood trees. It was like I'd entered a lavish resort. When I finally could see the mansion, I had to stop the car and gawk. It was if someone had built five large houses together into one mega-mansion. Four white columns framed the main entrance. In front of the mansion was a sparkling fountain surrounded by carefully sculpted bushes.

Behind the fountain were parking spaces that were obviously for visitors and I parked in one as the guard had instructed me. As I got out of my car, it dawned on me that I was only seeing part of the property. There must be acres of land behind the mansion. I knew professional athletes made tons of money, but the full extent of their wealth wasn't apparent until I saw this place.

I felt dingy in my Oxford shirt, jeans, and sneakers. Tucking my shirt in only alleviated my self-consciousness by a fraction. I pressed the doorbell and waited. A minute later, the maid answered the door and took my breath away.

The maid was Raegan.

She was dressed in a black and white French maid's uniform, the kind you'd expect to see at a Halloween party, not actually in use by a domestic servant. It had white lace trim around the neck and apron, a white lace ribbon waist cincher, and white ruffles along the hem of the dress. The hem barely covered her crotch. The black dress was cut low to show a generous amount of cleavage. I hadn't forgotten how fabulous Raegan's breasts were. They were pushed up so that they were two golden half globes threatening to spill out. Her black fishnet stockings were held up with black garters. Her high heeled shoes were black as well.

"Cole," she gasped. "What are you doing here?"

"I came to get you. I don't care what you've done, Raegan. I want you back."

She looked around nervously. "You don't understand. I can't leave. I have to stay here."

"Quintavious is the one who owes Rodney money. Not you."

"How do you know about Q?"

"That doesn't matter. The point is, I found you and I'm going to take you home where you belong."

Raegan put her hand on my chest. "I appreciate what you're trying to do, Cole. Really I do. I still care about you too. That's why I want you to get in your car and get the hell out of here before it's too late."

"I'm not scared of these people. All the money in the world doesn't give them the right to buy people."

"Actually, it does," said a smooth, deep voice.

Rodney Robinson stood in the foyer with a bemused look on his face. I'd seen him play on TV and I'd seen him play from the cheap seats, but it was still amazing to see him in person. He wore a purple velour tracksuit and the neon orange tennis shoes. I'd read that he was seven feet tall. He towered over Raegan and me. He sauntered across the polished floor and held out his hand. He had gold rings on his fingers.

"Mr. Blankenship," he said. "Welcome to my home. I'm Rodney Robinson."

"Of course you are," I said as I shook his huge hand. I expected a bone-crushing grip, but his was surprisingly limp. "I don't want any trouble, Mr. Robinson. I just want to take my wife home."

"Let's discuss this like civilized human beings. Come with me."

He led the way into the living room, though it was bigger than any living room I'd ever been in. Groups of chairs and sofas formed islands in the sea of beige carpet. A fireplace large enough to stand in dominated one side of the room. Rodney settled his long frame on to a plush sofa and motioned for us to join him. At least, I thought he meant both of us.

"Raegan," he said sharply.

She stood at attention. "Yes, sir."

"Get me a lemonade. You know how I like it. Cole, what would you like?"

It broke my heart to see Raegan treated like some kind of slave.

"A glass of water would be fine," I said.

Rodney nodded at Raegan and she hurried out of the room.

"Tell me, Cole," Rodney said. "Did Q happen to mention how much money he owes me?"

"No, he didn't."

"Two million."

I blanched. What sort of person makes that kind of bet if they can't pay it off? The answer hit me: the kind of person who depends on others to cover his debts.

"Then he should be here serving us drinks."

Rodney rubbed his chin. "Yes, he should, but Raegan volunteered her services. After some negotiation, she agreed to work for me for six months."

Cole did a rough estimate of how much that was per month. Maids didn't get paid that kind of money. Raegan had to be doing more than fetching lemonade and answering the door. Emily Ann had said she was a black cock hungry white slut. Obviously, part of Raegan's agreement with Rodney was that she be his whore for six months. And probably not just in Rodney's bed, but with every former and current NBA star who happened to stop in for a visit.

Picturing his precious wife giving herself to a parade of tall, black athletes made Cole sick to his stomach.

"Can't we work something out," Cole said. "Make a new deal?"

"Do you have two million dollars?"

"No, I don't have that kind of money, but I could set up a monthly payment. With interest. You wouldn't get it all back in six months, but soon enough."

Raegan returned. She carried a silver tray with two glasses on it. She handed Rodney and Cole their drinks. Cole realized his throat was very dry and took a big gulp of his water.

"Raegan, dear," Rodney said. "Please join us. Your husband has made an interesting proposition."

A look of shock spread across Raegan's face. She sat in a chair next to Cole.

"He can't do that," she said staring at me. "This is between you and Q. Cole has nothing to do with this."

"But Cole offered to make monthly payments. With interest."

"I think it's a fair offer," I said. "Considering the circumstances."

Rodney laughed. He had a deep throaty laugh that seemed to spread through his entire body.

"You come into my home and try to make a deal?" he said. His voice had gone from mocking to menacing. "This is some shit that don't even concern you."

"Raegan and I are still legally married, so this does concern me."

"Then why don't you take her place? You come work for me for six months."

"No!" Raegan shouted. "I won't let him. I made the agreement, not him."

"Let the man speak for himself," Rodney said.

Raegan turned to me and grabbed my arm. "Don't do it, Cole. I have the situation under control. It's much more dangerous here for you than it is for me."

I should have listened to her, should have read between the lines and heard what she was desperately trying to tell me. But I was bound and determined to be the hero and save my wife.

"What kind of work would I have to do?" I asked.

"It's the same deal Raegan made. You'd work as one of my servants for six months."

"He doesn't understand what that means," Raegan said.

"That's enough, Raegan. This is between me and Cole. I don't want to hear another word from you."

Raegan looked down at her lap.

"Come on," I said. "How hard can this job be? I should be able to handle it. I don't have to wear a maid's uniform, do I?"

Rodney leaned forward and smiled, revealing a gold-capped tooth.

"Only if you want to," he said.

"Definitely not."

"You do whatever it is I need you to do. That's it. That's the job."

"And if I agree to do this, then Raegan can leave?"

"Absolutely. However, if you quit before the six months is up, then she has to come back and work a full six months. Even if you work all but the last day."

I guzzled the rest of my water. I worked as a commercial insurance inspector. I was an independent contractor, so taking six months off would hurt my business, but it wouldn't ruin me. I hadn't been working lately anyway because I was so upset about Raegan leaving me.

"I'll do it," I said.

Raegan gasped, but didn't say a word.

Rodney fished his phone out of his pocket. He dialed a number. Whoever he called answered immediately.

"We have a deal. Please bring Mrs. Blankenship's personal effects to the living room."

I felt a stab of warning. What did he mean by "we have a deal?" Did he somehow know that I was going to offer to take Raegan's place? And if he did, how did he know?

Before I could ponder these questions any further, a tall black woman entered the room carrying a shopping bag and a woman's purse. The woman was stunningly beautiful. She wore a skintight red bodysuit that showed off her muscular body. She handed the bag and purse to Raegan, and then stood beside Rodney's chair.

"Well, Raegan," Rodney said. "You're free. You can leave now."

"Can Cole walk me out," she said. "I'd like to say goodbye."

"Absolutely."

"Let me drive her home" I said. "I need to go home anyway so I pack a suitcase."

"That won't be necessary," Rodney said. "I'll provide everything you need here."

"He's right," Raegan said. "I wore one outfit when I arrived." She held up the shopping bag.

"You're just going to walk out of here in that maid's outfit?"

"You can switch clothes with her if you like," Rodney said.

"That's really not funny anymore."

"It's all right, Cole," Raegan said. "I don't mind wearing this."

It was all happening so fast. I felt like I was falling into a deep well with no way to escape. I walked Raegan out of the house. I handed her the keys to my car. She threw her arms around me and we hugged. It was the first time I'd held her in my arms in months. I breathed in the sweet fragrance of her hair.

"I wish you hadn't done this," she said. "I'm not worth it."

"Yes, you are."

"You're a good man, Cole."

"Please don't go back to Quintavious. Promise me that you'll go home. Our home."

"And do what?"

"Wait for me."

We separated. Raegan had tears in her eyes. She put her palm against my cheek.

"I'll wait for you," she said. "Unless you tell me not to wait for you any longer, I'll wait for you."

Raegan got into my car and drove away. I turned and faced the mansion. Its shadow loomed over me like a whale about to swallow a minnow.

CHAPTER THREE
A ROOM WITH A VIEW

When I entered the house, the beautiful black woman was waiting for me. Rodney was nowhere in sight.

"Where's Rodney?" I asked.

"He's a very busy man. He had business elsewhere to attend to." She spoke with authority. I wouldn't want to piss her off. She held out her hand. "I'm Jerrica Jhones, Mr. Robinson's head of operations. Among other duties, I make sure his house runs smoothly."

Her grip was strong and firm, like a man's.

"So, my job is to do what you tell me to do," I said.

For the first time, she smiled. It was a lovely smile.

"That is correct," she said. "Come. I'll introduce you to your co-workers."

Meeting my co-workers included a tour of the mansion. As we walked the grounds, I realized that the mansion was actually a series of extravagant houses and buildings linked together. It was so vast and took up so much real estate; it was like being in a mini-city. I met the cooking staff, the cleaning staff, the lawn maintenance crew, the security team, and the auto repair shop. They all seemed to enjoy working for Rodney and greeted Jerrica warmly. She introduced me as Raegan's replacement to which they all smirked and snickered. I assumed that they thought it was funny that I was taking over for a maid.

The garage was the size of an airport hangar. This was where Rodney kept his cars. As we strolled through, I saw a Jaguar, a Maserati, an Aston Martin, a Hummer, an Escalade, a Tesla, a Rolls Royce, a Ferrari, and a Bentley. There were more but after a while they all began to blend together. Jerrica stopped by a Rolls Royce Phantom. It was black and elegant, much like Jerrica.

"One of your jobs will be chauffer," she said. "On those occasions, this is the car you'll drive."

"It's a beautiful car," I said. "I look forward to driving it."

"Don't get too excited. Rodney prefers to drive himself in one of his sports cars, but there are special events that require he arrive in a limo with a driver."

"So it's more for the optics."

"Precisely."

After the garage, Jerrica took me into a rectangular building that on the outside was almost identical to the garage. However, inside was a full size basketball court with an adjoining locker room, weight room, and showers.

"I see Rodney may have retired," I said, "but he brought the NBA with him."

"This is where he feels most at home."

We ended the tour in one of houses. It wasn't as big as the main mansion, but it was just as fancy. Jerrica led me to a bedroom on the second floor. It reminded me of an expensive hotel room I stayed in when I attended a convention in New York.

"This is where you'll stay when you aren't working," Jerrica said. She walked over to the closet and pulled the accordion door open. It was full of men's clothes. "These should fit you until I get a chance to have our tailor take your measurements."

"Take my measurements?"

"All of the staff's clothes are tailor made." She reached in and pulled out a chauffeur's uniform. "You can wear this if Rodney needs you to drive him before your own uniform is ready."

"Whose clothes are these?"

"Our former chauffer. He found employment elsewhere."

"And he just left his clothes behind?"

"He chose not to take them with him."

I could understand. At the end of my six months' servitude to Rodney, I didn't want to owe him anything. I planned to walk out of here in the same clothes I was wearing today.

"I see I have a TV, but not a computer."

"That reminds me, give me your phone."

I took a step back. "My phone?"

"Rodney is a public figure, which doesn't leave him much privacy. He fiercely protects what little he has left. That's why his staff isn't allowed to have a computer or a phone. He doesn't want to take the chance of you revealing details of his daily life. Ask anyone who has worked for a celebrity and they will tell you they had to do the same thing. Besides, you won't need your phone until you leave."

"What about my wallet?"

"This isn't a jail. Keep your damn wallet."

Reluctantly, I fished my phone out of my jeans' pocket and handed it to Jerrica.

"So what happens now?"

"Downstairs is the servants' dining hall. You will eat your meals there. Dinner will be served in two hours. I suggest you relax and make yourself at home. Watch TV if you like. I also suggest you go to bed early tonight. Breakfast is served at 7:00AM and then you'll go right to work."

"Will I see you at dinner?"

"No."

I waited for further explanation, but she offered none. She left, closing the door behind. I explored the room. In a dresser, I found boxer shorts, socks, and T-shirts. The clothes ran from fine suits to work clothes. I held a pair of pants up to my waist. The legs ended near my calves. The former chauffer was shorter than me. It was strange being among his things that weren't really his things. I couldn't get a feel for who he was because everything was chosen for him.

The only clues left by the former occupant of this room were in the air. In the bedroom, I picked up the scent of men's cologne, but in the bathroom I distinctly smelled women's perfume. So he had a girlfriend (or a number of girlfriends) who spent the night with him.

I looked out the window. I had a view of the swimming pool. It was a classic kidney shaped pool with a bathhouse next to it and plenty of chaise lounge chairs and tables with umbrellas. The water was crystal blue and the shadows of waves danced across the pool's concrete bottom.

It was early April a bit too cool for swimming, but there was a woman doing laps. Her powerful arms pulled her gracefully through the water. A large man with an equally large belly watched her from a chaise lounge chair next to the pool. He was black and she was white. He wore aviator sunglasses, a gold chain, and baggy shorts. She was naked.

She finished a lap and climbed out of the pool. The sun danced off her superb body. It was perfect with big, perky breasts, a tight stomach, a nicely rounded ass, and shapely legs. She grabbed a towel off the lounge chair next to her admirer and rubbed her long chestnut brown hair.

I couldn't hear what they were saying what with the window closed and the distance between us. The man said something that made her laugh. Then he said something else. She put her hand on her hip and they stared at each other for a minute.

She walked over to his lounge chair and held out her hand. He struggled to lift his oversized girth, but managed to get to his feet. Taking his hand, she led him to a chair that he could sit upright in. He began to sit down, but she stopped him. She undid his shorts and lowered them to the ground. His dick was enormous. It hung between his legs.

As he leaned down to kiss her, she stroked his dick. They kissed passionately. His dick grew erect. Their lips parted. She put her hands on his chest and directed him to sit down. She folded her towel, placed it on the ground in front of his feet and kneeled between his legs.

From my angle, I could only see the back of her head, so I couldn't see her put his dick in her mouth, but her motions were evident. Her head bobbed up and down while he leaned back. I wondered how much of his dick she managed to get into her mouth and then wondered why I would think of something like that.

I knew I shouldn't be watching them. Sure, they were engaged in a sexual act out in the open, but in the privacy of Rodney's mansion. I was the hired help spying on the owner's guests. I should turn away, close my blinds, and let them do their thing.

But I couldn't turn away. Maybe it was because it had been so long since I'd had sex with Raegan. I didn't even masturbate after she left. I was too depressed, too removed from my body to think about sexual pleasure. Watching this beautiful woman give this guy a blowjob gave me a tremendous hard-on.

I wanted to pull out my dick and beat off while I watched them, but that seemed not only wrong, but pathetic as well.

The man's expressions alternated between grimaces and smiles. I recognized those expressions. I'd made them myself when I was getting really good head. Her hands inched up his chest and tweaked his nipples. I couldn't take it anymore. I undid my jeans and pulled them down along with my boxer shorts.

I spit into my hand and rubbed my stiff dick. I was never into Raegan playing with my nipples, but watching the action below inspired me to reach under my shirt and twist one of my nipples. Between stroking my dick and pinching my nipple, my dormant sexual desire was coming back to life.

I fantasized that I was the guy in the chair and Raegan was kneeling between my legs. I loved her blowjobs. Most girls I dated in college only went down on me because they felt they had to. Because of their distaste for oral sex, they gave lousy blowjobs. But not Raegan. She loved sucking my dick and she loved when I came in her mouth.

The woman quickened her pace; her head bobbing like an engine piston increasing speed. I matched her speed on my dick. The man grabbed her head and pumped his hips rapidly.

I thought sure he'd keep going until he came in her mouth, but instead he pulled her off. She left a trail of spit from her lips to the tip of his dick. She got to her feet and climbed into his lap, facing him. He guided his dick to her pussy.

Once she was impaled, he grabbed her ass cheeks. They fucked like crazed weasels. Her sweaty tits flopped in his face. Her arms held onto his shoulders.

I could feel my balls contracting as I neared an orgasm. In that nether world of sexual desire where odd thoughts bounce around your head, Raegan was still in my fantasy, but I wasn't. She was screwing the black man.

Of course, that was why she was here. Maids didn't dress like a cartoon French maid. They dressed in loose clothes that could get dirty. Raegan was here to screw black guys like him. She was here to be a black cock hungry white slut.

That realization should have been enough to ruin my little sexual fantasy, but instead, I came harder than I had in years. I moaned as my sperm splattered on the windowpane. My legs shook from the effort of coming and coming. I couldn't stop. It felt so good to come after holding back for such a long time.

The black man came too. He moaned so loudly, I could hear him in my second floor bedroom. And then her moans joined his. His arms fell to his sides and his head tilted back. But, she kept riding his dick, no doubt coming all over his lap. I wondered if she wasn't another black cock hungry white slut. She probably had her own French maid's outfit.

I looked at my sperm dripping down the windowpane and felt ashamed of myself. I was about to get a towel from the bathroom to wipe it off when I heard clapping. Rodney was standing on the other side of the pool from the couple. The three of us were too focused on their sex act to notice his arrival.

The woman climbed off the black man and glared at Rodney. He stopped clapping and crossed his arms. The black man calmly stood and hiked his shorts back on. He waved at Rodney. Rodney waved back. The black man sauntered into the house.

The woman and Rodney stood at opposite sides of the pool. She clutched her breasts and puckered her lips in an obvious invitation. I'd never seen such brazen openness toward sex. Rodney turned away from her and walked into the house.

The woman shook her head. And then, she looked right at my window. I panicked and backed out of sight. Had she known I was watching the entire time or did she just happen to look in my direction? I waited half a minute before sneaking back to the window. The woman yanked a black string off the back of a chaise lounge. As she put it on her body, I realized it was a bikini, or almost a bikini. The black strips of fabric barely covered her nipples and vagina. She picked the towel up off the ground and wrapped it around her waist.

I was beginning to think she hadn't seen me after all, but right before she left the pool area, she looked back at my window and blew me a kiss. My heart skipped a beat.

I went to the bathroom, took a towel, and soaked it in the sink. I wrung out the excess water and came back to wash the sperm off the window. As I cleaned the window I wondered what kind of place was I in?

I took a shower and put on clean clothes. The pants looked ridiculous what with my calves showing, but at least they fit in the waist. I lay on the bed and watched TV. I felt exhausted. I should have felt exhausted. My entire life had changed in one day.

When it was time for dinner, I went downstairs to the dining hall. Nobody wore their uniforms so you couldn't tell what anyone's job was. I liked that. We were just folks at a job having dinner together. The cooks served us each an individual meal before they sat down with us.

I was served a steak with steamed vegetables. The woman next to me was served a large salad with oil and vinegar dressing. In fact, everyone had something different.

"Aren't you allowed to have what you want for dinner?" I asked the woman.

She giggled. "Don't I wish. Each of us is served food that will help us maintain the healthiest lifestyle. Since my job isn't as physically demanding, I'm given salads."

"That doesn't seem fair," I said as I cut a bite of steak. It cut like butter. The steak was seared on the top and inside it was as pink as a woman's vagina. I put it into my mouth and chewed happily. It was the best steak I'd ever eaten.

"I'm not complaining, they're great salads and I'm never hungry. But occasionally, I'd like to have a donut or a slice of pie." She nodded at my plate. "I see you have a very physically demanding job if they're serving you steak."

Suddenly, the steak didn't taste as wonderful.

Once everyone had gathered together, I counted the staff. Not counting me, there were ten members of the staff. Half this much staff would cost a fortune, so Rodney must be a member of the one percent. I could see it. He was paid millions to play basketball and then he appears in dozens of commercials. Then there are the endorsements and TV appearances. I was just seeing the domestic staff. No telling how many accountants and lawyers he had working for him. The man was an empire unto himself.

I kept expecting to see the woman with chestnut hair that I'd seen by the pool, but she never showed up. I guess like Jerrica; she didn't dine with us lowly servants. She might not even be a staff member. I felt like I'd seen the black man she was with before. He was probably some kind of celebrity if he was hanging out at Rodney's house. Maybe the woman was a celebrity as well.

All of the talk during the meal was about work. What needed to be fixed and what needed to be cleaned. What kind of events to prepare for? No one talked about personal stuff. No one mentioned spouses or children. Whenever someone finished their meal, they got up from the table and left. I hated that. It meant that this was going to be a very lonely six months.

I could do it. I was here for Raegan. I would endure for her.

CHAPTER FOUR
HARD LABOR

I don't normally eat breakfast. I usually have a cup of coffee and maybe a piece of fruit before going right to work. I don't like eating first thing in the morning. I wasn't happy when I stumbled into the dining hall at the crack of dawn desperate for a dose of caffeine and found a full breakfast waiting for me.

"What is all this?" I asked the server.

"Egg white omelet, turkey bacon, oatmeal, and a protein shake."

"Do I really have to eat this?"

"No one is going to force you, but trust me, you'll be glad you did. Besides, it's this or nothing."

"I've never worked anywhere where the employer decides your meals. Who is making the decisions on what we eat?"

"Jerrica. She used to be a sports therapist and a nutritionist for Rodney's former team. He hired her to work for him so I guess that makes us Rodney's team."

"But she does more than just plan our meals."

The server grinned. "She sure does."

I forced myself to eat the eggs and the oatmeal. I put off the shake until last. I thought sure it would taste like paste. It was an unnatural purple color. I took an experimental sip. It wasn't bad. I could detect berries and bananas. There was an aftertaste of something acidic, like grounded up aspirin that must have been the processed protein.

When I was done, a Hispanic man with massive forearms came over to my table.

"You Cole?" he asked.

"Yeah, that's me."

"You're with me today. Put on something you don't mind getting filthy dirty and if you got work boots, wear them. Meet me in the front of the building in thirty minutes."

I found some beat up clothes in a bottom drawer and a pair of work boots that were almost new. The boots helped cover the fact that the pants were too short. I made it downstairs in less than thirty minutes. The Hispanic man was waiting. He said his name was Aldo and shook my hand.

Aldo turned out to be a good guy to work with. He was very clear about our tasks and how to go about them in the most efficient way. Our job today was to build a fire pit. It involved digging up the ground, laying concrete, and lifting heavy stones. I'd done manual labor, but nothing like this. It was brutal. By the end of the day, every muscle in my body ached. I took a shower and went straight to bed. I slept like the dead until the alarm went off the next morning.

For the next three months, I worked every day with Aldo. Sometimes we had other guys working with us and sometimes it was just Aldo and me. We replaced a retaining wall that had been busted by tree roots. We tore down dead trees. We built an addition to the pool house. Whatever involved working outdoors and heavy lifting, we did it.

Aldo started each morning by growling, "We're gonna fix this bitch good today." I liked working with him. Unlike the other servants, he talked about personal things. He talked about soccer and his wife and five kids back in Ecuador.

"Rodney is a good boss," Aldo said. "He gives me food and a place to sleep for free. I send my entire paycheck to my family."

"He doesn't take any money out of your check to pay for room and board?"

"Not one penny."

Since I wasn't getting a paycheck, there was no way I could tell if Aldo was right about Rodney's generosity. As for Rodney, I never saw him. I had no way of knowing if he was even living in the mansion. He probably owned more than one residence. He could have been living at one of his many homes.

Busting my hump outdoors for three months left me tanned and in the best shape of my life. My body stopped aching. I had muscles where I'd never had muscles before. I even developed six pack abs. I thought about how surprised Raegan would be when she saw me.

By the time Jerrica finally arranged for the tailor to take my measurements, the former chauffer's clothes I was still wearing were loose on me. With only three months left in my obligation to Rodney, I didn't see any point in making me new clothes that I would be leaving behind. But then again, it wasn't for me to question how rich people wanted to waste their money.

The tailor was a middle age Asian man with round rim glasses. I stood in front of a mirror while he worked silently. Jerrica watched with her arms crossed. She was dressed in tailor made business suit. It was charcoal gray and managed to hug her attractive curves and still look smart and powerful.

"It'll be nice to have pants that cover my ankles again," I said.

"I need you to drive the Rolls Saturday night," Jerrica said.

She caught me by surprise. I'd gotten so used to working with Aldo every day that I'd forgotten that another one of my jobs was Rodney's chauffer.

"Saturday night. Got it."

"Your personal chauffer's uniform won't be ready by then, so you'll have to wear the former chauffer's uniform. Will that be a problem?"

"Nope. The boots will hide my bare calves."

"Don't you want to know where you're going?"

I shrugged. "I figured somebody would tell me some time before we reached our destination."

Jerrica laughed. It was a deep, throaty laugh. I liked it.

"You are the most pragmatic son of a bitch I've ever known. You remind me of Rodney."

I supposed it was meant as a compliment, but I didn't care much for Rodney. He could have let me pay off Quintavius' gambling debt with monthly payments, but instead he trapped me into six months of servitude. Not to mention that he had used my wife as a sex slave. No, being compared to Rodney was no compliment.

"Today's Wednesday," Jerrica said. "I don't want you worn out on Saturday, so I'm pulling you off the construction crew for the rest of the week."

"Any chance I could use one of my days off to go into town for a haircut?"

I usually kept my hair short in a near buzz cut, but when Raegan left me the last thing on my mind was maintaining my appearance. My hair was longer than it had ever been. It touched my shoulders and crept down my back. I'd been tying it into a ponytail, but I really wanted to cut this mess off my head. Long hair was a bitch when you're working in the sun.

Jerrica moved between the tailor and me. She held my ponytail between her fingers. I liked her perfume. It wasn't flowery.

"You have nice hair," she said. "We have a stylist who makes house calls. I'll have her come in Friday to cut your hair."

The next two days were like a mini-vacation. I slept in. I was still served the same damn protein shake at breakfast even though I wasn't doing manual labor. I spent most of my time in my room watching TV. I missed having my phone. I wanted desperately to call Raegan if only to hear her voice.

CHAPTER FIVE
LATE NIGHT VISITOR

I stood naked in front of the mirror staring at my reflection. I'm not a vain person. In the morning I only look at myself long enough to make sure there are no stains on my shirt and nothing between my teeth. But after three months working for Rodney, I could see changes in me and I didn't like them.

I might not have noticed the changes if it hadn't been for the stupid haircut. The stylist came on Friday. He had purple hair and was covered in tattoos. He brought his equipment in a rolling suitcase. I discovered that the mansion had a room built to be a small salon so that Rodney could get his hair done without leaving home. There were mirrors on all the walls and two chairs as well as sinks, capes, and even a barber's pole. The stylist, whose name was Kenny, set up his gear beside the first chair.

Jerrica sat in the second chair. I was glad she was there because I liked her company, but it bothered me that she felt it necessary to be present. There were times when the amount of control that she had over me was suffocating.

She and Kenny gossiped about their favorite reality shows why Kenny's scissors snipped my hair. When I suggested that he wasn't cutting it short enough, Jerrica told him to ignore me.

"Don't worry, Cole," Jerrica said. "You're going to look fabulous."

When he was finally done and turned the chair so that I could see the results, I was horrified.

"What the fuck?" I said. "This is a girl's haircut."

My hair flowed around my face in layers. It was still shoulder length only now it was more noticeable than before.

"I can fix that," Kenny said.

He scooped out globs of hair gel and ran it through my hair. When he was done, the top layer was spiky. All I needed was a ton of eyeliner and I would look just like David Bowie in "Labyrinth."

"It's still a girl's haircut," I said.

"It's not a girl's haircut," Jerrica said firmly. "It's the same haircut you'd see on all the men in the hottest clubs."

"Well, I wouldn't know about that."

"Then take my word for it."

After taking a shower so I could wash the goop out of my hair, I stood in front of the mirror to access my hair. I still thought it was a girl's haircut. The way it framed my face made me look almost like a girl. But then, I realized it wasn't just the haircut. My face did seem more feminine. It was rounder and softer. In fact, all of me was rounder and softer.

I still had the rock hard muscles and the flat stomach, but the six pack abs were more of a smooth belly. My legs seemed shapelier. Most shocking, my ass looked like a cute girl's tight ass. What was happening to me?

I got dressed and tried to think of an explanation. Could this possibly be how my body looks when I'm in my best physical shape? That didn't make sense. I'd been close to this pumped before back when I was in college and I was on the handball team. I was ripped then and there was nothing girlish about my appearance.

It had to be that damn protein shake. I was having a negative reaction and it was causing these side effects. I just had to explain it to Jerrica. The solution could be as simple as using a different brand.

When I went to dinner that night, I was given a much lighter meal than normal. I knew why immediately. Jerrica had adjusted my menu since I wasn't doing heavy labor with Aldo. Maybe that meant no more protein shakes. Maybe my problem had already been solved.

I spent the rest of the evening watching TV in my room. I went to bed early. I had no idea what kind of hours I'd be working tomorrow so I wanted to get plenty of rest. I lay awake for a couple of hours thinking about how odd my life had been these past months and then fell into a deep sleep.

I don't know how long he'd been in the room watching me sleep. He didn't try to wake me up. I woke up because I sensed his presence. He sat in a chair at the foot of the bed. I turned on the lamp on the bedside table.

"Aldo?" I said groggily. "What the fuck are you doing here?"

"I haven't seen my wife and children in three years," he said. "I miss them very much."

"Is that why you're here? To talk about your family?"

"I miss my wife most of all."

"I understand. I miss my wife too."

"I haven't touched her in three years. In all that time away from her, I have only been unfaithful one time."

"I know it's tough. It hasn't been three years, but I miss Raegan like you wouldn't believe."

He stood up and the light fell on his torso and his face was covered in darkness. I could see that he was clutching something in his hands.

"I try to be strong, but sometimes I am weak."

He moved closer to me. I could see that the thing in his hands was made of fabric. It had flowers printed on it. He held it up so I could see it more clearly. It was a peasant dress.

"This is my wife's dress," Aldo said. "Put it on."

I could feel the blood pounding in my head. I tried to think of ways to escape the room.

"Get the fuck out of here, Aldo," I said, sounding braver than I was. "Go to your room and jerk off if your need to, but leave me alone. I'm not into that shit."

He shook the dress at me.

"Put on the dress and nothing underneath. I will take you from behind. It will satisfy me enough that I can survive here another year."

"I told you I'm not into that shit."

"Don't play games with me. That's why you're here. Rodney will be mad if he finds out I fucked you first, so don't tell him."

My blood ran cold. Was he telling the truth? Was Rodney planning to sexually assault me? Was he that kind of pervert?

"Fuck Rodney and fuck you. Get the hell out of my room, Aldo."

Aldo dropped the dress and grabbed me. He dragged me out of the bed. I was wearing a T-shirt and boxer shorts. He tore the T-shirt off and tried to grab the boxer shorts. If he had attached me three months earlier, he would have had no problem overpowering me. His massive forearms would have held me helpless as he did what he whatever he pleased to me. But while I wasn't quite as strong as him, I was strong enough to hold my own against him.

If anyone had been walking down the hallway by my room, they probably would never suspect that two men were locked in heated battle inside. Other than a few grunts, we were silent. We wrestled on the floor, our bodies soon covered in sweat. He tried to dig his hand inside my boxer shorts and I pulled it away. He tried to get on top of me and hold down my arms with his legs, but I managed to push him off me. Our body odor filled the room in a heady stew of testosterone.

I thought I'd finally gotten him off me when he let out a savage growl, grabbed my stupid long hair and slammed my head on the floor. I saw stars and felt woozy. He did it again and I thought sure I would pass out. My body went limp and I felt like I was glued to the floor.

Aldo stripped off his shirt and pants. He wasn't wearing underwear. He pushed his erect dick against my mouth. I had enough control over myself to hold my mouth closed. The head of his dick poked at my lips. The earthy smell of it filled my nostrils.

"Just suck it, man," he hissed. "The other bitch thinks she's too good for me so it has to be you."

"Go to hell," I said through gritted teeth.

Aldo hung his head. His dick went soft and rested against my cheek. He climbed off of me, picked up the dress off the floor, and plopped down in the chair at the foot of the bed. He held the dress to his face and sobbed. He put the dress down and his face was etched with sadness.

"Lo siento, my friend," he said. "I lost my mind. I can't take it anymore. If I could just talk to Maria it wouldn't be so hard."

Here was proof that Rodney's no communication policy definitely had its downside. I got to my feet and felt the back of my head. I didn't seem to be bleeding though I was going to have a wicked headache. I leaned against the wall and folded my arms.

"What did you mean by saying that was why I was here?"

Aldo shrugged. "Everybody knew Raegan was here to fuck the black guys. I figured that's why you were here too."

It made sense, but I still had the feeling that he was lying.

"You said the other bitch thinks she's too good for you. Did you try to fuck Raegan?"

"No, man. Never." Then he thought about what he'd said. "Okay, yeah. That's what it was. I tried to screw her but she said she was too good for me."

Now I knew he was lying. Raegan might have turned him down, but she wasn't the type of person to say she was too good for someone, even if she thought she was. The question that worried me most was why was Aldo lying.

"Look, Aldo. It's late. Go back to your room and we'll pretend this shit never happened."

He hugged the dress to his chest. "It doesn't matter. I can't stay here any longer. I need to be with my Maria and our children. I don't care how good this job is or how much Rodney pays me. I'm packing my things in the morning and I'm going back home."

He gathered his clothes and bundled them with the dress under his arm. I really didn't want anyone to see him walking naked out of my room, but I wanted him out so badly it didn't matter. It was terrible that he tried to rape me. What was even more terrible was that I had gotten a hard on from all sweaty wrestling on the floor. I was as confused and conflicted at this moment as he was.

Maybe that was why after all that had gone down tonight, I still liked Aldo. He was in a shitty situation. Something I could relate to. He trudged out the door wearing nothing but sweat.

Once he was gone, I took a deep breath and exhaled. I went to the bathroom to see if I had any cuts and bruises. Other than a few minor scrapes on my arms, I looked fine. And I was still hard as a rock.

Rather than try to make sense of it, I pulled down my boxer shorts, squirted lotion into my hand, and stroked my hard dick. As I jerked off, I looked into the bathroom mirror. There was that girlish face and something else I hadn't noticed before.

I wasn't a hundred percent sure, I but I was pretty sure that my nipples were larger and the skin around them was slightly puffy, like little breasts. I pinched a nipple and it felt good along with the pleasure I was getting sliding my hand up and down my dick.

As I got closer to orgasm, I wondered what would have happened if I hadn't been able to stop Aldo. His dick would have been in my mouth and then in my ass. What would that have been like? How terrible would it have felt? Or how good?

Or how good? What the fuck was wrong with me?

On that thought, I came. Globs of sperm filled my hand and I continued to jerk my dick with the added lube provided by my spunk.

After the orgasm subsided, I felt sick to my stomach. This place was driving me crazy. Like Aldo, I needed to get out of here. I turned on the shower and waited for the water to get hot. I reminded myself that I was half way done. I just had to hold on a little longer.   I got into the shower and washed my sperm and Aldo's sweat off of me.

CHAPTER SIX
THE LIMO

Friday afternoon Jerrica sat down with me and went over my assignment for the night. At 9:00 PM, I was to be dressed in my chauffer's uniform and waiting by the Rolls Royce Phantom limo. She handed me a walkie talkie that it fit in the palm of my hand. Rodney had the matching walkie talkie. When he was ready to leave, which could be anywhere between 9:00 PM and 3:00 AM, he would contact me. I would then drive to the front of the mansion where he would be waiting. He would get in and tell me where to take him. When we reached the destination, I was to get out and open the door for him. He would go into the club and I would wait with the car in the parking lot reserved for limos.

"What if I have to take a piss?" I said.

"They have bathrooms for the drivers," Jerrica said. "And food if you get hungry. This is a very exclusive club. They don't just cater to their clients. They take care of their clients' crew as well."

When Rodney was ready to leave, he could contact me on the walkie talkie. I would then drive to the front of the club and open the door for him. The only time he wanted me to open the door for him was when others could see it. Otherwise, he could open his own damn door. He might want to come home or he might want to go someplace else for the night. When we got back to the mansion, I would drop him off at the front door and return the limo to the garage.

"Sounds simple enough," I said.

"It is," Jerrica said. "You'll do fine."

At 8:00 PM, I took a shower. As I was dressing, I decided I should put on something to make me smell better since we would be in the car together. I found a bottle of cologne that the former chauffer had left behind. It smelled expensive and I used it sparingly. I put on the chauffer's uniform, which included the military looking jacket with a double roll of buttons, a white dress shirt, a black tie, black slacks, driving gloves, and a black driving cap. I had to tighten the belt so the pants wouldn't slip down. The black leather boots covered my bare calves just as I thought they would. The driving cap looked silly on me, but at least it helped hide my long hair.

I entered the garage at 8:45 PM. I didn't want to lean on the car so I decided to sit behind the wheel. I ran my hand over the steering wheel. Every inch of the car felt expensive. The key was in the ignition. I started the car and familiarized myself with the controls. I turned off the motor and adjusted the rear view mirror.

Knowing there would be pockets of time where I would have nothing to do but sit on my ass and wait, I brought a paperback novel the former chauffer had left behind along with his clothes. I wasn't a fan of Western adventure stories, but beggars can't be choosers. I got to the part in story where the hero cowboy was lured into the saloon where four cattle rustlers were waiting to fill him full of holes when the walkie talkie crackled to life.

"Cole. We're ready." Rodney sounded like he was inside a metal tube.

I picked up my walkie talkie and pressed the talk button.

"On my way."

I started the engine and drove out of the garage and took the winding driveway that led to the front of the mansion. Rodney's few words hit me. He said, "We're ready" not "I'm ready." I wondered how many people I would be picking up. As I spun around the fountain, I got my answer. Rodney stood between the white columns of the main entrance. Standing next to him was the woman with chestnut hair I watched having sex by the pool.

She wore a skin tight dress that was hot pink and was so low cut, I could see her entire cleavage. Her hair was piled on top of her head and strands cascaded down to her shoulders. Her shoes were blood red spiked heels. Rodney wore expensive jeans, a white dress shirt, a black leather jacket, and black tennis shoes. They both wore gold chains.

Rodney held the passenger door open for the woman.

"Take us to the Gold Room," he said. "The address is saved on the car's GPS."

I fiddled with the GPS until I found the address. I drove down the long twisty driveway. I had a strange feeling as I drove through the front gate. This was the first time I'd been off the property since I came here. Glancing at the route on the GPS, I was reminded how far away Rodney's estate was from the city. I thought Raegan and I lived way outside the city in our suburban home, but we were much closer to downtown than Rodney.

"So you're the new chauffer," said the woman. She had a lovely feminine voice. "We haven't been properly introduced."

I looked at her in the rearview mirror. She winked at me and then smirked at Rodney. He rolled his eyes.

"Forgive me," Rodney said. "Somehow it slipped my mind. Cole, meet Penelope. Penelope, meet Cole."

Penelope leaned forward and hung her slender arms over the front passenger seat. Her perfume was so strong I wondered if she bathed in it.

"I like how you look in that uniform," she said. "You fill it out nicely."

"Thank you," I said.

"It's about time I got to see you, especially since you've already seen so much of me."

My cheeks burned with embarrassment. She knew that I was the one spying on her.

"I'm sorry," I stammered. "I should've minded my own business."

She ran a manicured nail down my arm. "I don't mind. I like to have sex and I don't care who sees me when I do."

"That's because you're a nasty little slut," Rodney said.

Penelope giggled. "Do you really think I'm a slut?" She teasingly asked Rodney.

"Damn right. You're addicted to dick. Can't get enough of it. You're a regular cum slut."

He pulled her next to him. I concentrated on the road. I expected them to raise the privacy window, but they didn't. Either they didn't care that I heard their conversation or they wanted me to.

There was another possible reason. I had smelled Penelope's perfume before- in the bathroom of my room. The former chauffer must have been one of her many lovers. Rodney may have been trying to warn me to stay away from her. Maybe he was tired of her screwing around.

He didn't have to worry about me. Even if Penelope was interested in adding me to her list of sexual conquests, I had no intention of getting involved with anyone while I was in Rodney's house. I wanted to do my time and leave.

"It's true," Penelope purred. "I can't get enough dick. But it has to be a big black cock. The bigger the better."

"Girl, you are so nasty."

"It's all your fault. You made me this way."

I could hear a zipper being pulled. I gripped the wheel tighter. We had left the country back roads as I pulled onto the freeway. I heard the rustle of fabric.

"There he is," Penelope cooed. "And he's happy to see me."

I resisted the urge to look in the rearview mirror. I could hear a wet smacking sound. I felt a bulge in my pants and scolded it for betraying me. They didn't seem care if I saw Penelope give Rodney a blow job, but I did. It made me uncomfortable and was a major distraction to my driving. I raised the privacy window and shut them out.

From the outside, the Gold Room looked like an industrial warehouse. A small neon sign on the brick wall read Gold Room. We had to wait in a line of limos to get to the entrance. When we finally arrived, I jumped out of the car and opened the passenger door. Rodney climbed out. From out of nowhere, paparazzi appeared. Their cameras flashed as they recorded his arrival.

Rodney held out his hand for Penelope. She took it and emerged from the back seat looking fresh and beautiful. Her lipstick wasn't smeared. No one would suspect that just a short time earlier, she was sucking Rodney's dick. Or maybe everyone in the club knew she was a slutty cocksucker and would have been more surprised if she hadn't gone down on Rodney.

As Rodney and Penelope entered the club, a rent a cop told me where to park the car. A section of the parking lot by the back of the club had been blocked off for limos. I found a space next to a dark blue Escalade limo.

The limo drivers' waiting room was a separate brick building. There were cheap couches and chairs, a TV tuned to a sports channel, bathrooms, a snack machine, and free coffee and bottled water. There were eight limo drivers in uniforms identical to mine lounging around the room.

There was a wall telephone and nobody was using it. I went over to it and picked up the receiver. There was a dial tone so the phone was working. I got ready to call home and see how Raegan was doing, but I hesitated. What if she wasn't there? What if a man answered? I brushed these worries aside. I knew in my heart that she was home alone.

I put the receiver back in its cradle, got myself a cup of coffee and took it with me back to the car. I didn't call because I wouldn't be able to say I was coming home. I would call her when I could.

I sat in the car, sipped coffee, and read the Western novel. The four cattle rustlers waiting to ambush the hero cowboy in the saloon didn't shoot him after all. Instead, they ganged up on him and beat him up. They left him for dead, but he was stronger than they suspected. He crawled to the doctor's cabin and the old sawbones patched him up. The recuperated hero cowboy had tracked down the rustlers and was about to get his revenge when my walkie talkie crackled and I heard Rodney's voice.

"Cole. Pick me up."

"On my way," I replied.

I checked my watch. They'd only been in the club for a couple of hours. I thought celebrities partied all night long. Not that I minded. It meant I would get to bed sooner than I expected.

Five minutes later, I pulled up in front of the club. To my surprise, Rodney was waiting by himself. There was no sign of Penelope. I got out and came around to open the door for him, but before I could, he opened the front passenger door.

"Get in," he said. "I'm going to drive and you're going to ride shotgun."

The paparazzi had a great time photographing the limo driver getting in the passenger seat while the sports celebrity got behind the wheel. I waited until we were out of the Gold Room's parking lot and on the road before I asked an obvious question.

"Where is Penelope?"

"I wanted to go and she wanted to stay, so her friends are going to give her a ride home."

Rodney turned on the radio. Hip Hop music blasted out of the speakers. He punched the channel buttons until he found a sports talk station. We listened to the Deejays argue over who would win the NBA finals. Rodney's name came up in the middle of the discussion.

"Again, the Pacers didn't make the playoffs."

"The Pacers haven't been worth a damn since Rodney Robinson retired."

Rodney didn't react. He kept his eyes on the road as he drove through downtown.

"It's true," I said. "Since you left, the Pacers have sucked balls."

"It wasn't my team," Rodney said. "I worked for the NBA and the Pacers were the team they told me to play for. I would have played just as hard no matter where I ended up. All I cared about was money and playing basketball."

"Sure, but it's nice to know that you were such a crucial member of their team." Rodney laughed. "Even if I had stuck around, the team would have gone to shit.

Management fired the head coach and traded away their best players so they could spend all their money on this basketball whiz kid going straight from high school to the pros. They think they've got the next LeBron James. The kid's good, but he's no LeBron. He can't carry an entire team."

Rodney pulled into a strip mall parking lot and slide the limo into the handicap space. He pulled a handicap hang tag out of the glove compartment and hung it on the rear view mirror.

"Why do rich people always act like the rules don't apply to them?" I asked.

"Because they don't," Rodney said. "Come on. And leave that stupid hat in the car."

I left my chauffer hat and jacket in the car and followed Rodney into a sports bar. There were at least a dozen TVs mounted to the ceiling, each tuned to a different game. The place smelled of beer and fried food. We found an empty booth and parked ourselves at it. A waitress in a tight T-shirt and very short shorts came over to take our order. If she recognized Rodney, she didn't show it.

"How you feel about a plate of hot wings and a pitcher of beer?" Rodney said.

I was shocked that he asked me. Actually, it was just dawning on me how odd this entire situation was. We were hanging out in a sports bar like a couple of old buddies instead of boss and employee. Or should I say boss and indentured servant.

"Wings and beer sounds great," I said. I mean what was I going to say?

The sports bar was a far cry from the Gold Room. We were way over dressed. Except for Rodney, there were no celebrities here. I'm sure people recognized him, but no one came over to ask for his autograph. The crowd was mixed. There were white people, African American people, men and women. Even a couple of Asians. They were united in their love of sports and chicken wings.

Our order arrived and we dug in. The wings were spicy hot, just the way I liked them, but it was the beer that made me a happy camper. I hadn't had alcohol for months. It tasted great.

I figured Rodney would want to watch the basketball game, but instead he concentrated on a soccer game. It turned out we were both Arsenal fans.

While we sat there, eating and drinking, and talking sports like two regular guys, I couldn't help wondering what he was up to. Why did he bring me here? It was obvious that he was more comfortable in a sports bar than in a high end night club, but that didn't explain my presence.

It was possible that he didn't have any friends and he needed his servants to keep him company. They say it's lonely at the top.

Two women stopped by our table. They both wore torn jeans, sports jerseys, and tennis shoes. One was black the other was white. Suddenly I realized the black woman was Jerrica. I didn't recognize her without the tailored suits and a backwards baseball cap hid her expensive hairdo. The white girl I realized was one of Rodney's maids.

"I bet Susie here that you'd leave the club and show up here an hour ago," Jerrica said as she put her arm around Susie's shoulder. "Now I owe her ten bucks."

Rodney laughed. "I guess I'm getting used to club life. You can join us if you'd like."

"No thanks. We're hanging with some friends over there." She pointed at a table of four women. They were dressed even more butch than Jerrica and Susie.

I wasn't surprised to learn that Jerrica was a lesbian. The truth was I never gave it any thought because it was none of my business.

"Tomorrow, we need to discuss personnel changes," Rodney said.

"Yeah, I got some ideas."

"Good. Let's meet after breakfast."

"You got it, boss."

Jerrica and Susie left to join their friends. Rodney turned to me. He made a steeple with his fingers.

"These personnel changes include you," he said. "Aldo gave me his resignation this morning so until I hire a new groundskeeper, you need to be reassigned."

"Why can't I be the new groundskeeper?"

"It's a long term job and you'll only be here for another three months."

"Good point." I refilled my glass from the pitcher of beer.

"But you have to stay in shape. I want all my workers to be in the best possible physical shape. It makes an impression on my guests. That's why I had you work with Aldo. I was sorry to see him go. He did amazing work."

I thought back to the other night when he tried to sodomize me and I managed to fight him off. I didn't see any point in mentioning it to Rodney. Aldo was gone and I'd never have to deal with him again. Still, I was sorry it ended the way it did. Until that night, I considered Aldo a friend.

"I guess I'll start working out," I said. "To stay in shape."

"Starting tomorrow, you'll begin working out under Jerrica's supervision."

"I'm guessing tonight is my last chance to drink beer for a while."

"That's right."

I took a long sip of my beer.

"Can I ask you a question?" I said.

Rodney smiled. He was a handsome man. If I were a girl, I supposed I would have been attracted to him.

"You can ask. Doesn't mean I'll answer."

"What's up with you and Penelope?"

"Why do you want to know?"

"I'm curious and I might as well try to find out something about the people who live next door."

"We tried to be a couple, but it didn't work out. We want different things."

"But she lives in your house."

"When she moved in I told her she could stay as long as she liked. The relationship may have died, but we're still close."

"How do you know Quintavious?"

Rodney grimaced.

"We grew up together in the hood. I got out, he stayed. We cross paths once in a while."

I nodded and drained my beer. There was more beer in the pitcher, but I'd had my fill. Drinking wasn't that big a deal to me.

"Can I ask you a question?" Rodney said.

"You can ask. Doesn't mean I'll answer."

The smile returned to Rodney's face.

"How did you and Raegan meet?"

"We met in college. Her sorority were the little sisters to my fraternity. We saw each other at the frat parties, but then we started seeing each other alone. After a few dates, I knew she was the one. We connected on a deep level."

Rodney nibbled on a wing and then wiped his hands with a napkin.

"I'm jealous. I've never felt that kind of connection with anyone. I guess that's what I wanted with Penelope, but the only connection she wanted was my dick inside her."

"It's weird to hear you say that."

"Why is it weird?" he said defensively.

"Most guys don't care about love. They just care about getting laid. For a lot of guys, Penelope is the perfect girl. She just wants to be a fuck buddy with no strings attached."

"Oh she's got strings attached to me. But I hear you about what guys want. I was that way for a long time, but now I'm older and I'm starting to want something more than to just get my dick wet."

"I hope you find what you're looking for."

He filled his glass and mine, emptying the pitcher. He held his glass up.

"Let's drink to that."

We clinked glasses and drank our beer. We hung out for another hour and argued about sports before Rodney drove us back to the mansion.

CHAPTER SEVEN
THE DRESS

"Ready to get your ass kicked?"

"No," I said. "But let's do it anyway."

Jerrica and I were in the gym. She had just led me on a four mile jog around the grounds. I was ready to hit the showers and call it a day and here was telling me that the jog was just a warm-up.

For the next two hours, she kicked my ass. She had me lift weights, run wind sprints, do push-ups and sit-ups along with other acts of torture. My T-shirt and shorts were soaked with sweat by the time we were done. I was proud of myself. I only threw up once.

Here I thought working with Aldo had whipped me into shape, but that was a walk in the park compared to the work-out Jerrica put me though. I barely made it. If my weak performance wasn't humiliating enough, Jerrica worked out with me and barely broke a sweat. She explained that she worked out every day and was glad for the company.

As we worked out, I had a chance to see how ripped she was. The girl was all muscle. Part of me wanted to be that ripped, but another part of me wanted to go back to bed. I had started to get ripped doing construction with Aldo, but then everything softened. That reminded me of my theory about the protein shakes. Jerrica still had me drinking them every morning.

"I think I'm having a bad reaction to something in the protein shakes," I said.

"Really?" Jerrica said. "Like a skin rash or stomach cramps?"

"No. More like my body is changing. My skin's softer."

"Are you turning into a girl?" she asked, laughing.

"Hey, I know it sounds crazy, but something's not right."

"Well, I haven't noticed any difference, but just to be on the safe side, I'll have the kitchen get another brand. If you're still having side effects after that, then we'll bring in a doctor to check you out."

I had to hand it to Jerrica. She took care of her crew.

After the work-out, I limped toward my building. Jerrica stayed behind, staring at her smart phone.

"Hey," she called out. "Just got a message from the tailor. Your clothes are ready. They're in your room."

"Finally, I can cover my ankles," I said.

In my room, I found the former chauffer's clothes had been removed and replaced with new clothes. I didn't want to go through them with sweaty hands, so I decided to take a shower first and then check out the new duds.

The hot water felt amazing on my sore muscles. I stood under the nozzle longer than necessary before soaping up and washing off the sweat. When I was done, I stepped out of the shower into a cloud of steam. The mirrors were fogged up. I toweled off and went into the bedroom.

It was silly of me, but I was excited about the new clothes. It was silly because they would only be mine for a few months. They weren't my clothes at all. They were the uniforms provided by my employer. Looking at how stuffed the closet was, I doubted I would get a chance to wear anything more than once.

I searched the dresser and took out a pair of boxer shorts and a white T-shirt. The T-shirt was tighter than I preferred, I liked them loose, but it wasn't uncomfortable. I looked at myself in the mirror and was horrified. I looked like I had breasts. Little bee sting breasts, but breasts all the same.

I ripped off the T-shirt and examined my chest. Sure enough, the area around my nipples was puffy. I could swear that my nipples were bigger and rounder. I touched them and they were sensitive. Maybe they'd always been this sensitive. I wasn't in the habit of feeling myself up.

I needed to find Jerrica and tell her about this right away. To hell with waiting. I wanted to see a doctor about these bizarre side effects.

I found a pair of pants and a shirt and dressed quickly. I stormed down to Jerrica's office, but she wasn't in. Her secretary informed me that Jerrica had left the grounds for a meeting and wouldn't be back until this afternoon. I told the secretary that it was urgent that I talk to Jerrica as soon as she returned. The secretary assured me that she would let Jerrica know and suggested I wait for her in my room.

I sulked back to my room and sat in the chair to wait. This was stupid. I had no idea how long Jerrica would be out. I decided to go through the new clothes.

I pulled out the new chauffer uniform and held the pants up to my waist. The legs reached my feet. Yay. No more naked ankles. I went through the rest. There were jeans, slacks, and khakis. Shirts, sweaters, and jackets. There were enough clothes for an entire year. Why did Rodney waste so much money on these clothes? The answer came immediately. Because rich people have more money than sense.

Buried in the middle of the closet was an item I almost missed. I felt it before I saw it. The fabric was silky smooth to the touch. I pulled it out. It was black and white. I'd seen one just like it before. On my wife.

It was a French maid's uniform with the black dress, white lace trim around the neck and apron, a white lace ribbon waist cincher, and white ruffles along the hem of the dress. My first thought was that somehow a mistake had been made. Someone else's dress had accidentally gotten mixed in with my clothes.

A heavy feeling in my stomach told me that this was no mistake. Rodney's people didn't make this kind of mistake. This dress was for me.

I had trouble breathing. After the way Aldo had trust his wife's dress at me, I didn't need this kind of bullshit. Did Rodney really expect me to wear this thing? There was no fucking way.

A second wave of panic rushed over me. Was it just the dress? I rifled through the closet. There were no other women's clothes in there. But women didn't just wear dresses. With a sickening realization, I searched the dresser drawers. In the bottom drawer, buried under shorts and sweats, I found them.

Black silk panties, a black bra, black fishnet stockings, and black garters were folded up inside a plain plastic bag. Under the bed I found a shoe box with black high heel shoes. It was the complete French maid's outfit.

I sat on the bed and tried to think. Aldo's words came back to me. "That's why you're here. Rodney will be mad if he finds out I fucked you first, so don't tell him."

Was Rodney planning on raping me? That didn't make sense. If he'd planned on attacking me, then why make sure I was strong enough to fight back? This whole situation was fucked up.

I hung the dress on the closet door and put the plastic bag containing the underwear on a hanger. And then I paced the floor for the next two hours. Finally, I heard a knock on my door.

"Come in," I called out.

Jerrica entered. She was wearing a business suit.

"What seems to be the problem, Cole?" she asked. She sounded peeved. Good. Because I was beyond peeved.

I pointed at the maid's outfit hanging from the closet door.

"Is this some kind of a fucking joke?" I said. "Because I'm not laughing."

Jerrica crossed the room to the closet. She lifted the hanger off the door and held the dress over her clothes. She looked at herself in the mirror.

"It found it sooner than I thought you would," she said. "Did you find the accessories?"

"They're in that plastic bag," I said.

"Have you tried it on yet?"

"Of course I haven't tried it on. So you admit, the dress wasn't put with my clothes by mistake."

She hung it back on the closet door and sat in the chair. She motioned for me to sit on the bed. Reluctantly, I sat down.

"The dress was made according to your measurements," she said. "It was made specifically for you."

"Why?"

"As a joke."

"A joke! Are you fucking serious?"

She held up her hands. "Calm down. Now, think back to when you agreed to take your wife's place here. You made a joke. You asked if you had to wear a maid's uniform."

I remembered that day clearly. How could I forget it?

"Yeah. I was making a stupid joke. It was a tense situation."

"And then Rodney told you that you would only wear the maid's uniform if you wanted to."

"Does he seriously think I want to wear that damn thing?"

She waved her hand dismissively. "No. Of course not. But remember who you are dealing with. Rodney is a jock. Were you ever on a sports team?"

"Yeah. I played basketball and football in high school. I played on my fraternity's basketball team."

"So you know how jocks are. They're constantly giving each other a hard time. Give them something to rag you about and they'll rag you about it for the rest of your life."

I could feel some of the tension leaving my shoulders.

"So when I made the joke about the maid's uniform, Rodney took it and ran with it?"

"Exactly. When it comes to teasing, nobody is worse about it than a professional athlete. They're already A+ personalities and they're super competitive. They live for this shit. It's stupid but effective. In fact, you could look at the dress as a compliment."

"Excuse me?"

"He remembered that stupid joke of yours and decided to pay to have a dress made to your measurements. Yes, this dress is a jock's way of showing somebody they like them enough to give them no end of shit. This is not the last time you'll hear about this dress. He's going to use it to fuck with you every chance he gets."

"Not if I burn the damn thing."

"He'll just have another one made. And another one after that. Push back enough and he'll replace your entire wardrobe with dresses. Best thing for you to do is to stick that thing in the back of your closet and forget about it. Every time he brings it up just laugh along with him like it doesn't bother you at all."

I started to feel ridiculous for making such a big deal, but then I remembered Aldo's late night visit. I felt comfortable enough around Jerrica that I could tell her about it. As I told her, her eyes widened and her mouth hardened.

"When he pushed his wife's dress at me and said that was why I was here; you can see why the maid's uniform freaked me out," I said.

"Absolutely."

"So why would Aldo say that?"

"Well, first of all, that's not why you're here. I think Aldo missed his wife so much that his mind snapped and he invented a reason to come after you. It was fortunate that he attacked you instead of one of the maids."

"How was it fortunate?"

"You had the strength to fight him off. A girl would have gotten raped."

As I let that one sink in, Jerrica stood. I got up too.

"Thank you for taking the time to talk to me," I said. "I know you're busy."

"No problem." She picked up the dress. "Let me put this away for you." She opened the closet, pushed all the clothes to one side, and hung it in the corner. Then she pushed the clothes back. I wouldn't see it unless I went looking for it. Then she opened the bottom drawer of the dresser, took out the shorts that were stacked inside, and placed them on the bed. She put the plastic bag with the underwear in it and the high heel shoes in the drawer. Then she covered them up with the shorts.

"I guess that takes care of that," I said.

"Remember, jocks have a stupid sense of humor," she said. "You want to know how stupid? The bra, panties, and shoes are in your size."

Mentioning the bra reminded me of why I wanted to see Jerrica in the first place. I needed to see a doctor about the puffy breasts I was growing. I was about to tell her as she was leaving the room, when she stopped, turned around, and snapped her fingers.

"Oh, I almost forgot," Jerrica said. "I talked to our food supplier and told them to get another brand of protein shake. They're sending it over today, so starting tomorrow you'll no longer be on that other stuff. If the side effects don't go away in a couple of weeks, let me know and I'll schedule you a doctor's appointment."

Damn, the girl was good.

"Thank you, Jerrica," I said. "Thank you for everything."

"Flattery will get you nowhere. I plan to kick your ass tomorrow morning just like I kicked it today."

CHAPTER EIGHT
HIT THE SHOWERS

I was leaving the weight room after my morning work-out with Jerrica when I ran into Rodney on his way in. He was dressed in baggy shorts and a sleeveless T-shirt. He'd been retired for nine years, but he was still in incredible shape with bulging muscles and oversized calves.

"Hey, Cole," he said. "Some of my old NBA buddies are coming over tonight. Why don't you join us?"

I was flabbergasted. Hanging out with professional basketball players? I mean, who wouldn't?

"Yeah, I'd love to," I said. "But I have to ask…"

"Why am I inviting the hired help?

"That's pretty much how I was going to phrase it."

"I want to make up for the prank I pulled on you."

I had to think for a minute before I remembered the maid's uniform. He had given it to me a month ago. I had forgotten that the damn thing was still in my closet.

"Well, it was a bit weird."

"What can I say? I have a weird sense of humor. So, come to the main house tonight around eight, eight thirty."

"I'll be there."

"And don't forget to wear the maid's uniform because you'll be serving drinks."

I froze. "What?"

Rodney laughed. "Sorry. I couldn't resist."

I forced myself to laugh along. And then, we went our separate ways. Not to overuse the word, but that was weird. The entire last month had been weird. For one thing, other than working out with Jerrica every morning, I'd done no work. After our work-outs I'd been spending the rest of the day exploring the grounds and marking my remaining time. With two months left, I was growing eager to get the hell out of this gilded cage.

Rodney hadn't asked me to chauffer him anywhere. In fact, today was the first time I'd seen him since we came back from our evening at the sports bar. He wasn't the only one I hadn't seen since that night. There had been no sign of Penelope.

At 8:15, I entered the main mansion. I could hear talking and laughter coming from the main living room. I entered and was speechless. Lounging on the couches, drinking cocktails and shooting the shit were four NBA legends. There was Kevin Franklin, four time NBA MVP; Lloyd Johnson, one of the greatest power-forwards of all time; Marcellus Underwood, selected to three All Defensive and five All NBA teams; and Sowande Chukwa, four time Defensive Player of the Year. And then there was Rodney making it five NBA legends drinking cocktails and shooting the shit.

"Hey, there's my man, Cole," Rodney said. "Let me introduce you to my friends."

I tried to say that there was no need to introduce me, but I was still speechless. Rodney introduced me to each guy and I shook hands with them. Their hands were so damn big and they towered over me. Watching these guys on TV, you know they're taller than average humans, but actually standing next to them, you realize just how big they are.

Somebody thrust a glass with amber liquid in my hand. I sipped it and tasted Bourbon. That worked for me. I joined the guys and listened to them talk. I answered direct questions, but I was too intimidated to join in.

Dinner was served by the pool. A grill had been set up on which they cooked tuna steaks and vegetables. We washed it down with more alcohol. Whenever I started to feel like these were regular guys, one of them would complain about an endorsement deal or brag about his next charity event.

"Who's up for a game?" Rodney asked.

"How we going to do this?" Marcellus said. "We only got five players."

"No, we got six," Kevin said. "Cole can play on my team."

"You sure about that?"

"Hey, I can beat you all by myself. I just need somebody to throw me the ball once in a while."

"What are we talking about?" I asked.

"We're going to play some basketball," Rodney said. "You didn't think I had that court built for looks, did you?"

There was no way I could play with these guys. They were pros. Besides, I hadn't played in years. And then there was the matter of our clothes. They were dressed casually, but that still meant expensive clothes and I was sure they didn't want to ruin them with excessive sweat.

"We're not dressed for basketball," I said. "My shoes would scrap the hell out of the floor."

"Not a problem," Kevin said. "Rodney keeps a supply of shorts, jerseys, socks, and jockstraps next to the locker room." He ticked each item off on his fingers.

"Plus enough shoes to open a Foot Locker store," said Marcellus.

Sowande put his arm around my shoulder. "Don't worry, man," he said. "It's all just fun and games. We don't even keep score. Don't tell me you never dreamed of playing in the NBA."

"In my wildest dreams," I said.

"Well, your wildest dreams are about to come true."

I had no more arguments. We sauntered over to the locker room. Rodney unlocked a side door that led into a large room. It was like stepping into the supply room for a sporting goods store. We each searched for our own clothes and carried them into the locker room. I chose an empty locker and kept my back to them as I changed. I was grateful that the puffy nipple side effect of the old protein shakes had worn off and my chest was back to normal. These guys would have teased me mercilessly if they saw me sporting mini titties.

Once we were done changing, we went out to the basketball court. Rodney turned on the lights. The polished wood floor gleamed. He rolled out a chart of basketballs and we warmed up, shooting baskets and stretching muscles.

"Enough fucking around," Rodney said. "Let's pick teams and play."

"I've already called dibs on Cole," Kevin said.

"Then I pick Sowande."

"Give me Marcellus."

"How come I always get picked last?" Lloyd said.

"I think you know the answer," Rodney said.

They all laughed, including Lloyd.

For the next hour, we played basketball. Or rather, I did my best to avoid getting trampled as they played basketball. I wasn't always successful. I got knocked on my ass a few times. A couple of times, I think they did it on purpose. But the guys seem to be doing it more to just see me on my ass than to hurt me. I did get the ball a few times and even scored a few baskets.

I'd enjoyed watching them play and do the amazing things they do on the court, but actually standing next to them as they did these incredible athletic feats was quite an experience. This more than made up for Rodney's teasing me about the maid's uniform.

"That's enough for tonight," Rodney said. "Time to hit the showers."

I had been on a number of sports teams and had showered with other guys after games dozens of times. I'd just played a friendly game with them so I was feeling a sense of camaraderie with the men. No alarm bells went off in my head when we stripped off our sweaty clothes and headed for the showers.

Soon the large tile room filled with the steam from our showerheads. I soaped up my body and felt the welcome sting of the hot water. We were clustered around each other. The guys were giving each other shit about how they played. We were in there a good ten minutes before I noticed their bodies. I wasn't in the habit at looking at other guys in the shower. I think most guys sort of train themselves to block out the nakedness. We might glance at a guy's cock and if it's a particularly crude group, we might make comments about its size or girth, but for the most part we look away.

But these NBA legends had magnificent bodies. They looked like they had been chiseled out of black Onyx. Their tall, muscular bodies didn't have an ounce of fat on them. And their cocks. Their cocks were enormous. Their balls were enormous. I have a respectable size cock, but they made me feel very small.

"Wanna touch it?" Lloyd said.

"What?" I gasped. "No, of course not. I don't know what you're talking about."

The guys laughed.

"It's okay," Lloyd said, moving toward me. "I don't mind."

"Yeah, yeah. You're real funny."

"I ain't kidding around. Touch my dick."

He kept coming toward me. I backed away. My embarrassment turned into fear. The other men edged their way toward me as well. As my back hit the shower room wall, I realized they had cornered me.

"Okay, enough fooling around," I said. "This joke is making me very uncomfortable."

"I already told you I wasn't kidding around," Lloyd said. "Now do as you're told and grab my motherfucking dick."

He snatched my wrist and pulled my hand toward his crotch. My fingers brushed against his cock before I managed to wrench free from his grasp. I tried to push between Sowande and Kevin, but they grabbed my arms and threw me back against the wall. I'd never felt more vulnerable in my life than standing wet and naked against a wall while surrounded by men bigger and stronger than me.

"Better do what he says," Rodney said. He glared at me as if I were an errant child.

Seeing no other choice, I reached out toward Lloyd's crotch. My hand was shaking as I wrapped my fingers around his massive cock. I was surprised that it felt velvety smooth.

"There, I touched it," I said, sounding braver than I was.

"Good boy," Lloyd said. "Now stroke it."

I looked at the other guys. There was a hunger in their eyes. I pumped on Lloyd's cock. It didn't get any bigger (how could it?) but it began to grow harder. I had never touched another man's penis before. I tried to pretend I was stroking my own, but that didn't work at all. My cock didn't feel anything like this giant snake.

"Not so hard," Lloyd said. "Take it slow and gentle. Now be firm. You're holding it like a little girl. Hold it like a man."

I followed his instructions. His cock grew harder. The other guys moved closer, tightening the circle. They stroked their cocks in rhythm with me stroking Lloyd. Everybody had a hand jerking them off but me. That was okay. I wasn't in the mood.

The room was silent except for the sound of hands slapping against thighs and stomachs as cocks were jerked off. The sound echoed off the tile walls and I noticed that showers had been turned off. At least we weren't wasting water.

Marcellus let go off his erect cock and it swung back and forth in protest. He grabbed my free arm and yanked it behind my back. Pain shot through me and I reacted by squeezing Lloyd's cock. He yelped and slapped my face. My cheek stung where he'd hit it.

"Watch it!" Lloyd growled.

"Sorry," I said weakly. Marcellus twisted my arm and the pain increased. "What's wrong? I'm doing what you told me to do."

"This is just a warning," he hissed into my ear. "It's time for you to get down there and suck Lloyd's dick. I don't want you getting ideas like using your teeth to hurt my friend."

"No, not that," I protested. "I'll jerk him off. I'll jerk you all off if that's what you want, but don't make me do that."

"You talk like you got a choice. Now get on your knees and put that pole in your pretty mouth."

He applied more pressure to my arm. The pain was overwhelming and I was spots. I was sure I would hear the bone crack at any moment. My legs were rubbery as I got down on my knees on the wet tile floor. Marcellus held onto my arm. Lloyd's black cock bobbed in my face.

"I'll do it," I said, "but first you have to let go of my arm."

"Why?"

"Please. Just let go of my arm."

"Do it," Rodney said. "It's not like he's going to get away."

Marcellus released my arm and I felt tremendous relief. As I rubbed my shoulder, I looked up at Rodney.

"Thank you," I said.

"Don't be too quick to thank me," he said. "For what we got planned, you're going to need both hands. Now get started on Lloyd's dick."

I wished I knew what he meant by needing both hands, but I didn't have time to think about it. Lloyd's cock was inches from my face. I slowly opened my mouth as wide as I could and went down on his cock. The spongy head slipped past my lips and into my throat. I gagged and had to pull away. I coughed, which made the men laugh.

"Try licking it first," Kevin said. "Then turn your head to the side so that it doesn't go straight down."

I did as he instructed. I licked the entire length of Lloyd's cock. I can't describe the taste, but there was something primal and familiar about it.

"That's nice," Lloyd said.

I turned my head to the side and went down on him again, but I gagged and had to pull out.

"I'm sorry," I said. "I can't help it. It's my gag reflex."

"Since this is your first dick, take it slow," Kevin said. "Don't try to stuff the whole thing down your mouth at once. That'll come later."

I nodded. I'd read that women who were raped often decided at a certain point to stop resisting. They even did whatever they could to please the rapist. The idea was that if they did what the rapist wanted, then it would be over sooner.

I made the same decision.

I put the head of Lloyd's dick in my mouth, but didn't go any further. I closed my eyes and concentrated on going up and down. Once I got past the gagging, sucking a dick wasn't terrible, but I still didn't like it.

Lloyd moaned so I must have been something right. He ran his fingers through my hair as I sucked on his humongous black cock. Saliva spilled out of my mouth and dribbled off my chin.

"That's good," Lloyd said. "Now suck my balls."

I hesitated and felt a slap on my butt. I could take a hint. Lloyd's dick popped out of my mouth. I stroked his cock which was lubricated with my spit and buried my head underneath it. I licked his nut sac and pulled one of his meaty balls into my mouth. His earthy sex scent filled my nostrils. I teased the ball in my mouth with my tongue and then switched to the other ball.

"Oh yeah!" Lloyd said. "This boy has talent. He's a natural born cocksucker."

I didn't wait for more instruction. I stopped sucking his balls and went back to sucking his cock. His big black cock. I ran my tongue along the shaft inside my mouth, which produced more moans of pleasure from Lloyd.

I had my eyes closed, so I didn't see what the other guys were doing. I assumed they were still jerking off as they watched me. But then, I felt something poking at my asshole. I pulled Lloyd's cock out of my mouth and twisted my head around to see what was going on.

"Hey, what are you doing back there?" I asked.

"Just getting you ready," Marcellus said. "Trust me, you don't want to get fucked without plenty of lube."

A lump of fear formed in my stomach.

"You're not serious, are you?" I squeaked.

His large finger entered my asshole. A new kind of pain coursed through my body and I fought the urge to bolt. I felt something slimy inside me. I tried to watch what he was doing, but he was right behind me. I heard the squirting sound when a tube is being squeezed. I felt something cold and gooey on my tail bone that trailed down my ass crack. Whatever it was, Marcellus stuffed it into me first with one finger and then with two. My body tensed at the invasion into my most private area.

"Hey, get back to work, bitch," Lloyd said.

I reluctantly turned my head forward and swallowed Lloyd's cock. It was hard to concentrate on Lloyd while Marcellus was doing who knows what to my ass. Marcellus' fingers must have been massaging my prostate because a tingling sensation spread from my ass to my cock. I could feel my cock stirring, which was the last thing I wanted it to do. If these guys saw me get a hard-on, they might get the wrong idea and think I was into this.

Lloyd must have gotten tired of the way I was blowing him, because he grabbed my hair with both hands and held my head still while he rammed his cock down my throat. I was caught off guard by his sudden attack on my virgin mouth. I tried to pull away, but he held on tight. I breathed through my nose as best I could and tried not to puke on his cock. All I could see what the curly trail of pubic hair that crawled from his crotch to his chest.

"Yeah, white boy," he panted, "Take that black dick. You know you want it. Don't you, white boy?"

As Lloyd face-fucked me, Marcellus continued to invade my ass with his lube-coated fingers. The other guys were crammed in close, their stiff black cocks waiting their turn. The smell of black man musk was so heavy; it was like a cloud floating around us.

Lloyd crammed his cock further down my throat. My nose nuzzled in his pubic hair as his balls bounced against my chin. His hard cock seemed to get even harder.

"Oh yeah," he groaned. "Here it comes. Swallow every drop, white boy. And then lick me clean."

I tried to protest, but with my mouth full of dick, my voice came out as a humming sound that seemed to delight Lloyd even more. I could feel his cock tense and then felt his sperm pumping through his shaft as it exploded down my throat. I sputtered as I struggled to swallow his huge load. His come leaked out of my mouth and coated my chin. His come tasted salty. I didn't like it, but I didn't mind it either.

As his orgasm subsided, Lloyd stopped gripping my hair and ran his fingers through it instead. The motion was sensual instead of rough and in some ways was worse than the raw power he'd exhibited over me a moment before. His tender touch treated me like a lover instead of a rape victim. Lover was the last word I would use for myself.

As instructed, I swallowed his load, licked his cock clean, and waited for whatever was coming next. I wasn't stupid enough to think we were done. There were still four more hard cocks waiting to come.

"I say he's ready," Marcellus said. "So, what do you say, Rodney? You want to be the one to pop his cherry?"

"That's okay," Rodney said. "You can go first."

"Oh no, man. You were the one who brought him in. Besides, he's your bitch. You should be his first."

"You're right. My handy man almost beat me to his virgin ass. When I found out, I fired him and had him deported."

Aldo was deported? Well, the bastard did want to go home. I realized that Aldo was telling the truth when he waved his wife dressed in my face and said this was the reason why I was here and that Rodney would be angry if he found out Aldo had fucked me first.

What was I thinking when I agreed to take Raegan's place? Never in my wildest imagination did I think I would end up on my knees about to get fucked in the ass after giving a fucking blowjob.

Rodney kneeled behind me. I could feel the head of his cock poking at my ass. I grimaced as I prepared for the agony that I was about to experience. He slapped my ass.

"Listen, Cole," he said in a soothing voice. "Whatever you do, don't tense up your asshole. Relax. Marcellus got you good and lubed so if you don't fight it my dick will slide right in like it belongs. Because, you see, my black dick does belong in your white ass. You may not believe that now, but soon you'll see the truth and you'll be begging me to fuck your ass."

His cock entered my ass and the pain was worse than anything I'd felt in my entire life. I let out a yell that echoed off the shower room walls. Rodney slapped my ass again.

"Relax!" he ordered.

I took a deep breath and tried to relax, but my arms and knees were quivering from the excoriating agony of his invasion of my ass. I prayed that he would pull out and get that baseball bat he called his dick out of me. Instead, he pushed in deeper. I didn't think the pain could get any worse, but it did. But only for a moment. Suddenly, his cock slid into me like it belonged. Just like he said it would. The pain eased off, but now I felt like I was stuffed all the way from my colon to my stomach. I knew he wasn't really in that deep, even with his super long cock, but that was how it felt.

"That's better," Rodney said.

His large hands gripped my hips and he slowly fucked my ass. A seed of pleasure blossomed somewhere deep inside me. My dick became erect. I cursed my body for betraying me.

Lloyd moved away from his position in front of my face and Sowande took his place. He held his black cock in his hand and smacked the side of my face with it.

"Don't want your mouth to get lonely while your ass is getting fucked," he said. "Now open wide and don't pretend like you don't know what to do."

I wrapped my lips around his cock and eased it down my throat. It was easier this time. I was beginning to figure out how to breathe and hold my head so that I didn't gag. The dire situation turned me into a fast learner. I gobbled his cock, coating it with spit. Then I licked the shaft before nuzzling my nose between his legs so my mouth could get to his balls.

"Damn, Cole," Sowande said. "I'm impressed. You are already a number one expert cocksucker."

Rodney panted as he quickened the pace of fucking my ass. His groin slammed against my ass checks as his thrusts grew more urgent. His grip on my hips tightened. I was under his complete control.

"That's it, bitch," he said. "Take that dick, bitch. You're my white bitch. Your ass is mine."

His words should have sent shivers of dread through me, but his cock was doing something to me and I was consumed with desire. I sucked Sowande's huge black cock faster and faster. He moaned and played with my ears. I managed to look from side to side. Lloyd was idly stroking his limp cock while Kevin and Marcellus were making out. For some reason, seeing those two NBA legends kissing like lovers was more shocking than everything that had happened to me so far.

Professional sports were dominated by macho, heterosexual men. I was sure gay men played on the teams since the dawn of the professional sports, but you rarely got a gay man to admit he preferred men. I was watching them act out their hidden desires. I wasn't bothered by the fact that they were gay. I just wished they hadn't forced me to join them.

"I'm going to come," Sowande announced. "Hold your mouth open."

I waited for his hot salty sperm to fill my mouth. To my surprise, he pulled out and pumped his cock furiously. It dawned on me what he was about to do seconds before he did it. I held my mouth open as he instructed as he shot his load. Most of the gobs of gooey white made it into my mouth while the rest splattered my face. His spunk stuck to my forehead and my cheeks. I'm sure some of it ended up in my hair.

"Well done, Cole," Sowande said. "Now lick me clean."

As I licked the leftover sperm off his cock, Rodney dug his fingers painfully into my sides. He groaned loudly and I felt his seed fill my ass. He seemed to keep coming and coming as his body shook with his sustained orgasm.

It was a great relief when his cock finally slipped out of my ass. My hard-on grew soft as well. I could feel his come dripping out of my bunghole. I curled up on the floor which was still warm from the hot shower. I felt dirty and used. I had endured all I could endure. I was done.

But they weren't done with me.

I looked up. They circled me with their cocks pointing at me. Rodney reached down his hand and helped me to my feet.

"I can't take anymore," I said.

He just smiled.

Rodney put his arm around my shoulder and led me out of the shower room. We went to the weight room. Kevin and Sowande stacked blue exercise mats in the middle of the floor.

"Lay down," Rodney instructed. "On your back."

I don't know why lying on my back scared me more than being on all fours like a dog. I think it was because when I was on my hands and knees, I couldn't see a lot of what was happening to me. Now I would be forced to see it head on. Plus, the position was too intimate and too feminine. A man on top of me.

"No, I won't do it," I said.

Rodney punched me in the jaw. The hit came so quickly I didn't have time to react. The room spun and went black. When I opened my eyes, I was face down on the mat. My head was fuzzy as strong hands easily turned me over onto my back.

As I regained focus, Marcellus knelled at my feet. He had a wicked grin. He pushed my legs apart and bent them back toward my body, exposing my ass. Rodney handed him a tube of lubricant. He squirted it between my legs and used his thumb to work it inside me. He guided his huge cock to toward my ass. I braced for the horrible pain that I knew was approaching. Though I was still sore from Rodney reaming me earlier, Marcellus' cock entered without causing me any pain. Rodney's giant cock must have stretched out my asshole.

Marcellus grabbed my ankles as he plundered my ass. Kevin got on his knees and turned my head to the side so that his cock was inches from my mouth.

"Open wide!" he said.

I did and he crammed his cock into my mouth. Marcellus continued to fuck my ass. As I tried to keep up with the two of them, someone grabbed my hand and placed it on their throbbing cock. I took my mouth off Kevin's cock so I could turn to see what was going on. Lloyd was on my other side. He was already hard again.

Kevin jerked my head back toward him.

"You can suck me and jerk him off at the same time," he said.

I did my best to service the three men simultaneously. I didn't want to get punched again. They'd made it clear. If I didn't do what they wanted, then I would pay a price. They were bigger and stronger than me. And there was five of them to just one of me. I had no choice.

But that wasn't the worse part. The more contact I had with their big black cocks, the more I craved them. Their velvety smoothness, their rigid need, and their overpowering scent were intoxicating. Part of me wanted desperately to run away and hide until this foreign desire was out of my system and another part of me wanted this night to go on forever.

I couldn't understand where this desire was coming from. I'd never been attracted to men. I'd never had forbidden feelings for a guy. There was a dull ache in my head from Rodney's punch. Maybe I was delirious from the blow. Perhaps I wasn't thinking clearly. Or maybe I had convinced myself that the best way to survive was to enjoy the ride.

Or maybe I really liked big black cocks and just didn't know it until I had one rammed up my virgin ass.

Luckily, my dick didn't stay hard. Instead, it flopped up and down in rhythm to Marcellus thrusting his cock into me. We were all slick with sweat and the room smelled heavier of sex than the shower room had.

Even though I was only on my second round of man on man sex, I could sense the men's orgasms. The smell grew more intense. I could almost feel their balls contracting. I prepared to swallow Kevin's seed and for Marcellus' hot spunk to fill my ass. I wasn't sure what to do about Lloyd. Maybe I would have time to catch his sperm in my mouth after Kevin came.

"Man, Cole, you are one sweaty son of a bitch," Kevin said. "You're getting all slippery."

"You're right," Lloyd said. "This boy needs a bath. What do you say, Rodney? Should we give your boy a bath?"

I'd forgotten about Rodney. He was standing a foot away, watching the action through heavily lidded eyes.

"Yeah," he said. "Give the boy a bath."

As if on cue, the three black men pulled their cocks away from my mouth, ass, and hand. They grabbed their respective cocks and shot wads of creamy come onto me. They coated my face, chest, and stomach with their sticky seed. Then, they rubbed it all over my body. I was covered in come.

Laughing, they got to their feet and went into the shower room. I started to rise, but Rodney pushed me back down on the mat. He plunged his cock into my mouth as Sowande stuck his cock into my ass. They fucked me until they came in me instead of on me.

For the rest of the right until the early morning, the five men took turns putting their cocks in either my ass, mouth, or hand. I couldn't believe they could get hard again so quickly or had so much come stored in their bodies. Come leaked out of my ass until I was lying in a puddle of communal spunk. My stomach was so full of come I felt like I'd eaten a seven course meal. In a way, I had. My hands ached from jerking off their cocks. I tasted my own shit and lost all pretense that I wasn't enjoying what they were doing to me. I gobbled their cocks hungrily and thrust my hips to meet their massive black cocks. I wrapped my legs around their torsos like a desperate lover.

As terrible as my descent into this sexual depravity was, the very worst was yet to come. It was the last fuck of that long night. Everyone had left but Rodney. He mounted me and I wrapped my legs around him and locked my ankles behind his back. He started slow, which just caused me to want his cock more. I tried to quicken the pace to bring his hot seed inside me, but he forced me to slow down. He leaned down close to me and placed his lips on mine.

Until this moment, nobody had tried to kiss me. I was their slut. You don't kiss sluts. The intimacy shook me to my core. This was too much. This was beyond rape. He wasn't treating me like his victim. He was treating me like his lover.

For the sake of my sanity, I should have turned away. I kissed him back. And then we were kissing with open mouths and tongues exploring each other's throat. He was tasting the sperm of all his friends. I was tasting him. The real Rodney. We embraced as we kissed more passionately than I ever remembered kissing Raegan.

His fucking increased in speed and I equaled his savage thrusts. He reached down and grabbed my dick. It stroked it with urgency. I realized stupidly that I had been building up desire all night and had been given no relief. Now he was offering it. It wasn't right. I didn't want him to make me come. If he did, then he would have something precious of mine. Something I wasn't ready to give to another man.

But it had been such a long night and their big black cocks had teased me so mercilessly. I had a raw need for release.

Rodney continued to kiss me and stroke my dick as he fucked my ass.

"Can you feel it?" he said. "I'm about to come. Will you come with me?"

"I can't. I shouldn't."

"Aren't you beyond can't and shouldn't? Give it to the pleasure. Give yourself to me."

"No."

"Yes."

He pounded me with greater intensity. His hand felt so damn good on my dick. A heat was rising inside me. I could feel my balls contracting. It was beyond my control. I was going to come whether I wanted to or not.

"I'm coming," I screamed.

"So am I," Rodney said.

His body convulsed with his orgasm. My dick erupted and I came on his stomach. I came harder than I ever had before. When his cock softened and slid out of my ass, I felt empty, drained of everything inside me.

I stood on wobbly legs. I was numb from all the abuse I'd endured. But I was determined to show Rodney that I had taken his worse abuse and survived it. I was going to show him how tough I was.

"Is that the best you can do," I said.

And that was the last thing I remembered.

CHAPTER NINE
THE BITTERSWEET TRUTH

I woke up in my bed. I don't know how I got here. Someone must have carried me. I wondered if it was Rodney. The idea of him cradling my abused, naked body in his arms sent a shiver down my spine. I felt both disgusted and a slight stirring in my balls. I peeked under the covers. I was naked, but at least I wasn't covered in sperm. Somebody had bathed me. Thank God for small favors.

Everything ached. It hurt to move. My throat felt raw. My breath was atrocious. Nothing hurt more than my ass. I wondered if I was bleeding. Like a woman on her period. I felt my jaw and tried to decide if any teeth were loose. I would have gone into the bathroom and checked my face and body for damages, but I was too humiliated to look in the mirror. I wanted to hide from the world.

And more than the humiliation, I was scared to death because of the part of me that enjoyed it. I didn't enjoy it the entire time. In the beginning, I hated it. But then at some point those big black dicks felt so good inside me and I craved their hot salty come in my mouth. My body betrayed me and I hated myself for it.

I had to get out of this place. Today. If I stayed and they came for me again, what if I liked it a little bit more? And after that, a little more again. And again until I craved it. What would I become? I didn't want to think about that possibility and I didn't have to because I was definitely leaving.

The bedroom door opened and Jerrica entered.

"Look who's finally awake," she said cheerfully. "I let you take today off, but I want to see your lazy ass back in the gym tomorrow morning."

"There's not going to be any more workouts," I said, struggling to sit up. "I'm leaving."

She plopped down in the chair next to the bed.

"Really?"

"Something happened last night with Rodney and his NBA buddies. I can't stay here another day. I'm leaving and you can't stop me."

"You got your cherry popped last night."

It felt like the temperature in the room dropped by 50 degrees.

"You knew this was going to happen." It wasn't a question. It was an accusation.

"What the hell do you think you're training has been for? I had to get you in shape so you could hang with them dudes. So, was it everything you hoped and dreamed it would be?"

I was flabbergasted. She was saying terrible things as if it were no big deal.

"I don't understand. When did Rodney decide he was going to rape me?"

"When Q called to say you were on your way over here to rescue Raegan. The way he figured it, you wouldn't have gone to all that trouble if you didn't want her to take her place. Of course, he didn't make his final decision until he met you. Then he was convinced that you wanted this as much as he did."

My head swam and I thought I would pass out again. I laid my head on the pillow.

"He's wrong. How did he get such a crazy idea?"

Jerrica moved from the chair to the side of the bed. She touched my cheek. I should've brushed her off, but she was the closest thing to a friend that I had in this madhouse.

"You really thought you were rescuing Raegan, didn't you?" she said.

"Of course. Why else would I have agreed to stay here?"

"And what did you think you were rescuing her from?" When I didn't answer, she answered for me. "You didn't want to do what you were forced to do last night. The thing is deep down you knew they wouldn't have had to make her do it. You knew she was a hardcore black cock hungry white slut and that made you crazy. Maybe even made you a little jealous too."

"Jealous? Fuck no!"

Jerrica grinned. "Rodney told me everything, including how hard you came. Don't you see? It all worked out the way it was supposed to. If Raegan had stayed, nothing would have happened."

"I am so fucking confused right now. Please explain what the hell is going on."

"Well, you probably figured out by now that Rodney is bisexual. The other four gentlemen you met last night are like me, full on gay."

"Yeah, I noticed."

"Yep. They're faggots. Homosexuals. You know how hard it is to be gay in the NBA? The few professional athletes who've come out of the closet saw their careers seriously crippled. So they had to keep it a secret. And then there's freaks like Rodney. He likes pussy and dick, but most of all he likes chicks with dicks."

"Chicks with dicks? Like transvestites?"

"You got it. He's the master at finding a boy who wants to be a girl who is dominated by a superior man. The way he sees it he's just freeing the girl inside."

"And he thinks I want to be a girl? That's bullshit. I have never wanted to be a girl."

"Then he read you wrong. Problem is, it's too late now. He's determined to break you in."

"Well that's too fucking bad because like I said before, I am leaving today."

"You can't leave yet. You got two months left to pay him back Q's gambling debt."

"He can sue me. And when he does, I'll tell the world about his kinky sex habits and how his NBA buddies are all fags."

Jerrica picked up the TV remote from my beside and turned on the TV. She pressed some buttons and a video played on the screen. From the high angle, it appeared to be a surveillance video. I sat up in the bed and my mouth went dry. It was from the weight room last night. The video was incriminating enough, but there was audio too. To anyone but those involved, it looked like I was completely into having sex with the three men grunting over me. Jerrica had picked the moment when Lloyd, Kevin, and Marcellus came on me at the same time. I don't remember hungrily licking their jizz off my face. To make matters worse, their faces had been blurred out. Only my face was clear.

"Let's make a deal," Jerrica said. "You don't tell and neither will we."

"This is blackmail."

"Yeah, I guess it is."

I know it's okay for men to cry, but I never cry. Even at my father's funeral, I didn't cry. I wanted to cry right then.

"What would have happened if I hadn't taken Raegan's place?" I asked.

"She would have done her six months and gone home to Q. To be honest, she was pretty bored. Rodney's gay friends wouldn't touch her. Rodney is friends with a lot of rappers who stay here from time to time and they like pussy, but Penelope was fucking them, so that left Raegan with nothing else to do but to actually be a maid."

"She tried to warn me. She said she could handle being here better than I could. Why didn't I listen to her?"

Jerrica turned off the TV. "I keep telling you it's because it was meant to be. By the way, Rodney's glad that you chased off Penelope. He was getting sick of her shit."

"What are you talking about? I didn't touch Penelope."

"It's not anything you did. She's always been a jealous bitch. She didn't mind you wearing her old clothes for months, but she couldn't stand that Rodney was paying more attention to you than her."

My stomach lurched. I scrambled out of bed and ran to the bathroom. I just made it to the toilet bowl before I puked my guts out. Most of it was sperm which grossed me out and caused me to hurl again. As I washed my face and brushed my teeth afterwards, I forced myself to look in the mirror. The side of my face was purple where Rodney had punched me. There were bruises on my arms and legs. I looked like hell.

I stumbled back to bed. Jerrica was waiting for me.

"Penelope?" I said.

"She was the chauffer before you. When we hired her, her name was Glenn. Rodney had no trouble turning her. Once she got a taste of a big black cock, she was hooked for life. Unlike you, I didn't have to hide her estrogen treatment in a protein shake."

"So there was something in those damn shakes." I looked down at my puffy nipples. "I think I'm going to be sick again."

"You need to hug the porcelain bowl again?"

"No. I'll be fine. Tell me more about Penelope."

"She went complete transgender and talked Rodney into paying for her operations. So now she's got tits and a pussy and a constant need for black dick. Rodney tried to have a real relationship with her, but she didn't want to be tied down to just one dick. She wanted them all. He had succeeded too well with her and didn't know how to deal with it. He let her live here because he felt responsible for her, but then you came along. She got jealous and went to live with Dawgie Daddy."

"Who?"

"Don't listen to a lot of rap music, do you?"

"Sorry, no."

"Big time rapper. You saw him fucking Penelope on your first day here."

"Oh that guy."

I stared at the ceiling. What was I going to do? I didn't want to end up like Penelope. But I didn't want that video of me to get out either.

"I'm screwed no matter what," I said.

Jerrica spread out next to me on the bed. She found my hand and squeezed it.

"It's not as bad as you think," she said.

"No, it's much, much worse."

"You just have to survive the next two months. That's eight weeks. And then you can go back to your old life."

"A lot can happen in eight weeks. I don't think I can endure another night like last night. I think I might kill myself instead."

"Don't talk like that. Admit it. Part of you was into it last night."

"That's what worries me," I said, choking back the tears. "I don't want to become like Penelope. I want to stay who I am. I don't want to lose myself."

"I told you, Penelope was into it from the start. Look, for a brief period of my life I dated a guy. I didn't hate it. It was nice. But in the end, I realized that I preferred women. It can be the same thing for you. For eight weeks, you let your freak flag fly and then you go back to being regular old Cole. Once you stop taking the hormone pills, your body will return to normal. I promise. The experience might even spice up your sex life with Raegan."

"I just don't know, Jerrica."

"I can help you. I can teach you how to play the part. I can teach you how to take dick the right way so it's not painful. You just have to trust me and do what I tell you to do."

"How can I trust you? You haven't exactly been honest with me so far."

"You're right. But if you don't let me help you, the next two months are going to be hell. And if you do let me, then the only danger is you might like it too much.'

"I'm damned if I do and damned if I don't."

"Then you might as well get some pleasure out it."

I squeezed my eyes shut. I had to be strong. I would be strong. I was Cole Blankenship now and I promised myself that I would still be Cole Blankenship two months from now.

"Okay," I said. "But I'm still not going to wear that fucking maid's uniform."

"That's the spirit," Jerrica said. "First things first. How attached are you to your body hair?"

"Which body hair are we talking about?"

"Facial hair, leg hair, underarm hair, ass hair, arm hair, pubic hair, most of your eyebrows. It's all got to go."

"Good lord, what have I done?"

"I haven't even gotten to the butt plug yet."

"The what???"

CHAPTER TEN
COLE'S NEW BEST FRIEND

"Meet your new best friend."

Jerrica Jhones held up a black object. It had a wide middle that tapered into a thinner blunt top and a flared stand at the bottom. I found out later that it was made of silicone.

"What is it?" I asked.

"A butt plug."

"What am I supposed to do with it?"

"What do you think? It goes in your butt. Duh."

"Are you kidding me? It's huge. There's no way it's going to fit in my ass."

"Don't worry. We'll start with these smaller ones and work up to this one."

She took out a small plug and a medium size plug that were identical in shape and color to the larger one.

"Remind me why I'm agreeing to do this?"

"So it doesn't hurt the next time something like this goes in your ass."

Jerrica took out a dildo and slammed it on the table. It was a very real looking black cock that was long and thick. My butthole ached at the memory of the big black cocks that were shoved into it recently. If stretching out my asshole in advance helped ease the pain the next one of their cocks entered me, then I was all for it.

We were in a spacious room in a secluded corner of NBA legend Rodney Robinson's mansion. The room was a cross between a product showroom and a sexy boudoir. It was ultra-feminine with red velvet wallpaper and pink plush wall to wall carpeting. The smell of roses hung in the air. Ornate cabinets were filled with everything the pampered sissy would need: make-up, hair products, perfumes, nail polish, sexy underwear, lingerie, high heel shoes, stockings, garter belts, falsies, anal lubricants, dildos, butt plugs, hormone treatments, and other assorted items that I couldn't identify. I sat in a comfy chair while Jerrica took items out of the cabinets and placed them on a display table between us as if I was shopping for these things.

I reminded myself that I only had to do this for eight more weeks, and then I could return to my normal life. And back into the arms of my beloved wife, Raegan. I was doing this for her. I just hoped that I would still be the man she married when it was all over.

"Here's something else you'll need to become familiar with," Jerrica said. She held up a red rubber bulb with a white nozzle. I recognized an enema bulb, though I'd never used one.

She didn't need to explain why I'd needed to use it. When the five ex-NBA players used me as their personal sex toy, their cocks traveled my ass to my mouth many times. I tasted enough my own shit to know that I wanted a clean colon as much as they did.

There was a knock on the door. I tensed up. I didn't want anyone outside of Jerrica and Rodney to know I was in here. Jerrica answered the door. Two petite Asian women entered the room. Each carried a large canvas bag over her shoulder.

"Cole," Jerrica said, "This is May and Jing. They're here to remove your unwanted body hair."

"Who says I don't want it," I said.

"Okay, Rodney doesn't want it."

"As long as we're clear about that."

A door on the other side of the room opened into what I can only describe as a salon. There were two salon chairs, a pedicure station, sinks, showers, and bathrooms. It was twice as big as the room where I'd had my hair styled. I wondered how many more rooms like this were in the mansion.

"Take off clothes," May said.

As I began to disrobe, so did they. They took off their matching Polo shirts and skinny jeans, but kept their bra and panties on. They were seriously cute and I felt the beginning of a hard on. Nervously, I stripped down to my boxer shorts.

"This too," Jing said, pulling on the elastic of my shorts and letting it snap back.

I pulled them down and covered my crotch with my hands. They opened one of the canvas bags and pulled out shorts and tops. They put them on and stuffed their other clothes into the bag.

"I see you're in good hands," Jerrica said. "I'll come by to check up on you later."

She disappeared and I was alone with the two women. They ignored me as they set up their equipment. When they were ready, May stood in front of me.

"Take shower first," she said.

I'd taken a shower that morning, but decided it wasn't worth arguing. I got into the shower and bathed. Jing handed me a fluffy towel when I was done. I don't know whether it was the shower or the women's all business attitude, but my erection had faded away and my dick hung quietly. Which was a good thing because May and Jing didn't let me put anything on.

They laid out towels on one of the salon chairs that folded out into a narrow bed. They had me stretch out on the bed. Using lotions, razors, and tweezers the women removed most of my body hair. When they were done, my chest, back, butt, legs, underarms, and face were hairless. They plucked my eyebrows until they were two thin lines on my face. Then they went to work on my nails and my toenails, buffing, trimming, and cleaning them.

I'd never felt more naked and exposed in my life.

They were about to pack up their equipment when Jing pointed at my crotch.

"We didn't do his pubic hair," she said. "He still hairy down there."

They trimmed my pubic hair, examined their work, and then decided it was better to just shave all the hair off. May squirted a mound of shaving cream into the palm of her hand and spread it around the base of my dick and around my balls. I about had a heart attack when I saw Jing come toward me with the razor.

"Don't worry," May giggled. "We done this hundreds of times. We haven't cut anything off yet."

"Unless you want us to cut it off," Jing said.

"No," I choked. "I'm rather fond of them."

With expert precision, Jing shaved around my dick and my balls. May held my dick so that Jing could get at everything easier. May gently moved it from one side to the other. The shaving cream made the shaft slippery so even though she held onto me tightly, her hand moved up and down.

The combination of her firm grip and Jing's razor scrapping the sensitive skin around my balls made my heart beat faster and sent confusing signals to my brain. I was scared shitless and sexually excited at the same time. My dick grew erect in May's hand. As if the day hadn't been embarrassing enough, now this had to happen.

"Does that feel good?" May asked.

"Sorry," I said. "But yes, your hand feels very good."

"We are not ladyboys. We are real girls."

She ran her fingertips along the length of my shaft sending tingling sensations down into my clean shaven balls.

"You ever been with a real girl before?"

Jing wiped the excess shaving cream off my scrotum, but May held onto my dick. They must have thought I was gay and grossed out by women. I wonder where they got the idea? Could it be because I was in sissy central with a personal set of training butt plugs?

I could see no reason why Jerrica would have told them my story. They probably had discreetly shaved a number of men transitioning into Rodney's bitches. They assumed I was just another sissy in training. I thought about correcting them, but May's hand on my dick felt so amazing that I decided to say nothing.

"You should try sex with a real girl with a real vagina," Jing said.

"You might like it," added May.

"You really think so?" I said, trying not to laugh.

Jing and May looked at each other and a silent decision was made. Jing ran to the door and locked it. She and May wiggled out of their clothes. Jing had firm little tits and the cutest ass I'd ever seen. May was curvier with medium size breasts. They both had jet black hair with matching black pubic hair.

May moved her hand to the tip of my dick and licked the shaft. Once she got it good and slick with her spit, she gently stroked me as she buried her head between my legs. Her tongue tickled my balls. Since they'd just been shaved, they were extra sensitive. I gripped the armrests of the chair and moaned.

Jing grabbed my head and pressed it between her breasts. She didn't have much but I didn't care. I sucked on her left nipple until it was erect and then moved on to her right nipple. She ran her hands through my hair and I suckled her.

She pulled away so that she could adjust the chair. She lowered it so that it became a flat bed. Then she climbed on and straddled my face. Her pussy smelled delicious and I dove right in. My tongue found her clitoris and teased it while I grabbed her firm ass.

"You've done this before, haven't you?" she said.

I answered by swirling my tongue around her pussy. She moaned and played with her nipples. Meanwhile, May shifted from licking my balls to sucking my dick. Her warm mouth felt incredible and I fought the urge to come right away. I hadn't been with a woman in months. And I had never had two women at once. I was determined to make this last as long as possible.

With Jing sitting on my face, I couldn't see what May was doing, but I felt her mouth leave my dick and then the pressure of her body on my legs. Her hand grabbed my dick again and then a moment later, I felt my dick enter her pussy. It had been too long since I'd been inside a woman. It was heaven. I moaned with pleasure, which vibrated into Jing's pussy.

Jing climbed down and I could see May as she rode my dick. Her eyes were closed as she planted her palms on my chest. Jing got back on but turned the other way so that faced May. I licked her pussy while she and May kissed above me. The room filled with the sweet smell of people fucking.

I was humping along happily when suddenly both women dismounted. They hunkered down together at my knees. Jing sucked my dick while May licked my balls. Every red-blooded boy dreamed about doing two chicks at once, but to actually be on the receiving end of two gorgeous mouths servicing your dick at the same time was amazing. I was about to lose my mind it felt so damn good.

Jing switched from my dick to sucking on my nipples. Raegan had sucked on my nipples a couple of times, but I was never a fan of it. But thanks to the hormone treatment Jerrica had me on, they were enlarged and extra sensitive. They were almost too sensitive as I felt waves traveling from my nipples to my toes.

May leaned her torso against my crotch as she positioned my dick between her breasts. I'd said they were medium size, but they were big enough to cover my dick. The combination of Jing sucking my nipples and May titfucking me brought me to the edge of orgasm. Somehow I managed not to blow my load.

"Hey," Jing said. "I haven't had any dick yet. You've been hogging it."

"Have not," protested May. "Get it on if you want to."

May moved aside.

"Get up," Jing said to me. "I want you on top."

Who was I to argue? I got off the chair and Jing lay down in my place. She spread her legs as I climbed on top of her. May guided my dick into Jing's pussy. She was sopping wet and I slid in easily. Her pussy was like an inferno inside. We had just gotten into a matching rhythm when she gritted her teeth, clenched her eyes shut, and her body convulsed. I'd never seen a woman come so hard. Her fingernails scratched at my chest as her orgasm ripped through her body. I could feel her pussy gripping my dick, trying to pull everything out of me. But still, I managed not to blow my load.

"Don't stop," Jing panted. "Keep going. That was just the first one."

Our bodies were slick with sweat as I pounded into her. I forgot all about May until I felt her hands reach between my legs. She fondled my balls as I worked Jing to her next orgasm.

Jing's body tensed as she prepared to come again.

"Yes, yes, yes," she cried.

As her orgasm reached its full strength, May inserted her finger into my ass. I lost control and blew my load into Jing's pussy. Her vaginal muscles drained every drop out of me and there was a ringing in my ears. When I finally caught my breath, I struggled not to collapse on top of the petite woman.

I slid off of Jing and sat next to her.

"You not a sissy boy," Jing said. "You like pussy too much. Why you here?"

"It's a long story, but I have to be here."

"You may like pussy now, but you won't later if you stay here," May said.

"We've seen manly men come here and leave girly girls," Jing said.

They didn't need to tell me. I'd met Penelope.

The three of us showered together. May was the only one of us who hadn't had an orgasm so Jing and I ganged up on her. I massaged her clitoris while Jing sucked on her nipples. Hot water wasn't the only thing that caused steam to rise in the shower.

May turned her back to me so that I could enter from behind. I held onto her hips and slammed into her pussy while she made out with Jing. When she came, her screams echoed off the walls. I pulled out and came on her ass. The water washed my sperm away.

And then, we soaped each other's body and rinsed off in the hot water. I exited the shower feeling completely refreshed and royally fucked. After we toweled off, the women put on the clothes they arrived in. I couldn't find mine.

"Have you seen my clothes?" I asked.

"Jerrica took them," May said.

"What the hell am I supposed to wear? I can't walk around naked."

"Plenty of clothes in the other room," Jing said.

My stomach dropped as I thought of all the women's clothing in the next room. For the next two months, that was my wardrobe.

"Wait here," May said. "We go tell Jerrica that we're done.'

They gave me lingering goodbye kisses both on the lips and on my dick. And then they were gone and I sat alone in the salon. Fifteen minutes later, Jerrica poked her head in the door.

"You decent?" she said.

"If sitting here buck naked is decent, then yes, I'm decent," I said.

She came in, had me stand up and turn around. She ran her fingers against my smooth hairless chest.

"They do good work. But if they expect me to pay them extra for fucking your sorry ass, they're in for a rude surprise."

CHAPTER ELEVEN
COLE'S FIRST BRA

Jerrica and I left the salon and went back into the boudoir. I was past feeling weird about walking around naked though I shivered because of my lack of body hair.

"Lean over the table," Jerrica said, pointing at the presentation table. "I'll do this the first time, but now on, you'll have to do it yourself."

It was like getting a prostate exam from a doctor. Jerrica put on rubber gloves, lubed my asshole, and inserted the smallest butt plug.

"Keep it in there for the rest of the day," she said.

"What if it falls out?"

"Put it back in."

"What if I have to take a shit?"

"Then take it out and then afterwards put it back in. Damn, do I really have to explain this shit to you?"

I looked at the open cabinets filled with women's lingerie.

"I guess I have to get used to wearing this stuff," I said.

"This stuff? No, we got something better than this," Jerrica said. She took out a satin blue bathrobe with black lace trim and handed it to me. "Put this on for now and follow me."

I put on the robe. It came down to just below the tip of my dick. We were on the first floor of the main mansion. I wasn't familiar with this house since I'd spent the last six months working on the grounds and living on the second floor of the servant's house. The main mansion was a labyrinth of hallways and large open rooms, winding staircases and endless hallways.

I followed Jerrica to a grand staircase up past the second floor to the third floor. She threw opened double doors to a huge bedroom. The closets were filled with women's clothes. There was a walk-in closet just for shoes. The bay window looked out over the lush grounds. The bathroom had a tub and a shower.

"This is your new room," Jerrica said.

"Wow," I said. "It's a life size Barbie dream bedroom. Seriously, girls who played with Barbie dreamed of growing up and living in a room like this."

"All the clothes and the shoes were custom made to fit you."

"Rodney has a thing about buying tailored clothes."

"He does indeed." Jerrica straightened the lapel on her suit jacket.

"Let me see if I have this right. The boudoir is where guys are introduced to the sissy lifestyle and from there they graduate to their own room?"

"Yeah, but since you're not here that long, we had to move you from the boudoir to your own room on the same day."

I cringed. "This isn't Penelope's former room, is it? I already lived in her room when she was Greg."

"No. This one was made up just for you. Penelope's room is across the hall, should she ever decide to come back."

As soon as I put on women's clothes, I was crossing a line. I just hoped I could cross back. I inspected the closet. The clothes were slinky and soft to the touch. The overall style was sensual and extremely feminine. Then, I saw it. Shiny black fabric with white lace trim. I yanked it out of the closet and threw it on the floor. It was the maid's uniform.

"What the hell is this doing here?" I demanded.

Jerrica laughed. "You didn't think he was going to let it go, did you?"

My face burned with embarrassment. Of course, Rodney wasn't going to stop taunting me with this stupid dress. He was having too much fun annoying me with it. The worst part was that it didn't seem like a jock picking on a buddy. It seemed more like a guy teasing a girl he had a crush on.

"I should throw it out," I said. "Or burn it."

"Don't do that," Jerrica said. "He'll take it as a challenge and go overboard, like replacing all your clothes with maid uniforms."

Jerrica picked up the dress and held it against me.

"With the right make-up you could pull this off," she said.

"She's right, honey. You got the legs to really rock the naughty French maid look."

Jerrica and I turned to see who had joined our conversation. An attractive woman with large blue eyes and wavy blonde hair wearing a navy blue pantsuit stood at the open double doors.

"I'm sorry I'm late. I would have been here sooner but I got lost in the mansion. I forgot about the endless hallways to nowhere. The architect who did this place should stick to designing mazes for amusement parks." She focused her blue eyes on me and rushed toward me with her hand extended. "You must be Cole. I'm Monica. We're going to have great fun together."

She gave me a firm handshake and then stood there grinning at me. I was dumbstruck.

"You're right on time," Jerrica said. "Cole's session with the salon girls ran long." She turned to me. "Cole, this is Monica Selling. She's a transgendered woman and an old friend of Rodney's. I asked her if she'd be willing to mentor you and lucky for us, she accepted."

"I'm confused," I said. "I thought you were mentoring me."

"It takes a village to turn a man into a woman," Monica said.

"Monica's joking," Jerrica said, "but in a way she's right. I can only guide you to a certain point, and then you need someone like Monica. She understands this process better than me because she's actually experienced it. Also, you're not the only person in this house that I'm in charge of. I got shit to do, girl."

Jerrica gave Monica a hug and marched out of the room. Alone with Monica, I looked at her more closely. She didn't appear as if she'd ever been a man. She certainly didn't smell like a man. If Jerrica hadn't told me, I would have sworn she was born a woman.

"Do you mind if I take a look at what I'm working with?" Monica said.

I hesitated. Monica was a complete stranger, she wanted to see me naked, and she wasn't my doctor. Yet something about her made me trust her and I took off my robe and revealed my shaken body. She walked around me. As she went behind my back, her fingers lightly grazed my smooth ass. I felt a tingle that went to my ears and my toes.

"How does the butt plug feel?" Monica asked.

"Okay, I guess."

"May and Jing do excellent work. Your body has reacted well to the hormone treatment. You're still a long way from passing as a woman. You're a little too tall and your hands a bit too big, but I've worked with bigger lugs than you and turned them into beautiful swans. Okay, I've seen the merchandise. Let's play dress up."

The first thing Monica did was show me how to put on underwear. I never realized how complicated a bra could be. She showed me how to put it on and adjust the straps. The bra was made for crossdressers and included hidden pockets to hold silicone inserts. The panties were also made for crossdressers. Monica showed me how to tuck my dick for a seamless look.

When she was done, she had me look at myself in the full length mirror. I was shocked. Just wearing bra and panties made me appear more woman than man.

From there, she instructed me on how to put on a garter belt and stockings. She helped me pick out clothes so that went best with my kind of body shape. She spent a good two hours teaching me on to put on make-up.

The most difficult lesson of the day was learning how to walk in high heels. I wobbled painfully for an hour before I finally began to get the hang of it. I never realized that being a woman was so fucking hard.

"Okay," Monica announced. "That's enough for the first day. But before I go, let's take another look at you."

I stood in front of the mirror again, but now I was fully dressed in a black dress, black stockings, black high heels, full make-up and red lipstick, and my hair teased. The silicone implants in my bra made me appear to have a nice set of hooters. I didn't just look like a woman. I looked hot. I looked like the kind of woman I'd want to fuck.

The room spun and Monica had to help me sit down on the bed before I collapsed. She went into the bathroom and came back with a glass of water. I took a sip and noticed that I'd left lipstick stains on the edge of the glass.

"The first time you get the full impact can be overwhelming," Monica said.

I broke down and cried. I cried like a little girl. Monica held me as I sobbed on her shoulder. She patted me and told me everything would be okay.

I explained why everything wouldn't be okay. I didn't know how much Jerrica had told Monica, but I went over my whole story, about Raegan leaving me, about coming here to rescue her, about having to take her place, about getting raped by five black men, and ending up dressed as a woman with a butt plug in my ass.

"Since the day we married seven years ago, I've been faithful to my wife, but then in the last two days I've had sex with seven people. Five black men took me against my will and then I fucked two Asian women."

"So, you don't want to dress up as a girl?"

"No! But if I don't do this, Rodney will show the world that video of me."

"Is it really that bad?"

"It is. The worst part is that you can't tell I was forced to do it. It looks like I'm into it. I get sick just thinking about it."

Monica wiped my tears away and taught me how to reapply make-up after a good cry.

"So what if Rodney releases that video," she said. "If you don't want to be here, then leave. Come on. We can go now. I'll take you anywhere you want to go."

"No," I said, shuddering. "I can't. My life will be ruined if that video gets out."

"Ruined? Really? Sure it'll be embarrassing and for a few months black guys will hit on you, and then everybody will forget about it."

I looked down at my hands. Monica had also shown me how to put on nail polish. My nails were a shiny blue color. I buried my face behind those beautiful nails.

"I'm so confused."

"You are so curious about what this life might be like, you can't bear to leave. The only person forcing you to stay here is you."

"I feel like I'm losing the real me."

"Or discovering the real you. I think you owe it to yourself to find out. Have you ever had an urge to put on women's clothes before? Maybe you tried on a pair of Raegan's panties when she was at work?"

"Never."

Monica narrowed her eyes at me, but didn't argue.

"You've had a big day," she said. "I'll tell Jerrica to have your dinner sent up here. You need some alone time. I'll see you tomorrow."

She gave me a kiss on the cheek and hugged me before she left. I got undressed and took a long shower. Afterwards, I got under the covers of the bed naked and stared at the ceiling. Or rather I tried to stare at the ceiling. My gaze kept drifting back to the closets. Finally, I gave in and put on the bra and panties. I tried on different dresses.

I liked the feel of the fabric on my skin. I liked how they hugged the slight curves of my body that I'd developed as a result of the hormone treatments. I tried on different shoes and tottered around the room in each pair.

A knock at the door caused me to about jump out of my skin.

"Who's there?" I called out.

"It's Susie. I've got your dinner."

Susie as in Jerrica's girlfriend, as in the maid. I cracked open the door. She was in her maid's uniform, a real uniform that wasn't at all like the French maid fantasy outfit in my closet, and she had a rolling cart with covered dishes. I let her in. She rolled the cart to the center of the room.

"Jerrica has a message for you," Susie said.

"Okay."

"Be at the gym by the usual time. You still have to work out every morning."

"What the hell am I supposed to wear?"

Susie giggled. "I'm sure there are workout clothes somewhere in this room."

I looked around. "I'm sure you're right. Okay, I'll find them and see her in the morning."

"You can just leave the cart in here. Somebody will get it tomorrow. By the way, you look very nice."

Her comment was sincere, but it flustered me. I muttered a thank you. Once she was gone, I picked at my food but I wasn't hungry. I searched the closets and drawers and found women's workout clothes in my size along with a pair of pink tennis shoes. At this point I wasn't surprised that everything was in my size.

I washed the make-up off my face, removed the butt plug and cleaned it, and brushed my teeth. I was exhausted and wanted to sleep, but now I had to decide what to wear to bed. I found flimsy nighties in a variety of colors. Raegan wore an old T-shirt and a pair of men's boxer shorts to bed. But I was supposed to dress more girly, so I put on the black nightie and got into bed. The nightie was more comfortable than I expected. Before I knew it, I was asleep.

CHAPTER THIRTEEN
SLEEPING BEAUTY

I dreamed of swirling yellows, aqua blues, purples, and pinks. Glitter fell like snowflakes. Giggling echoed in his ears. A crown hovered in the air. I jerked awake. The room was dark. The clock on the nightstand read 3:00AM.

The dream brought back a memory that I had long buried away. I was seven. Mary Beth lived next door. We played together all the time, but I wasn't invited to her birthday party. The party theme was princesses and boys weren't allowed. Mary Beth asked her mother if I could come anyway. Her mother wanted to please her daughter and probably didn't see any harm in dressing me in her daughter's clothes. I liked how the clothes felt on me. They were also more colorful than my boy clothes. I had long hair, lots of boys did back then, and I looked like another adorable girl at the party.

We were given glittery crowns and fairy princess gowns. We spun in circles so the gowns were swirl around our legs. There was a lot of giggling and too much sugar. Really, other than the clothes, it wasn't much different from any other kid's birthday party I'd attended. I had a great time.

When the party was over, I changed back into my regular clothes, went home, and pretty much forgot all about it. A few weeks later, Mary Beth's mother showed my mother photos from the party. Mom had no idea I'd gone and she certainly didn't know I'd gone dressed as a girl. Mom freaked out, but not near as badly as Dad did. I was forbidden from playing with Mary Beth. The bad feelings between my parents and Mary Beth's parents got so bad, we moved away and I never saw Mary Beth again.

I was left with a mixture of shame and sadness. I was sad because I missed my friend. The shame was more complicated. I wouldn't have felt ashamed if my parents hadn't freaked out. I probably would have forgotten all about the party. Or maybe I would have ended up where I am tonight, wearing a nightie and a pair of silk panties, but sooner.

The shame also brought a thrill. I had been caught doing something naughty even if I wasn't aware that it was naughty. I buried the thrill away along with the memory of the party. I hadn't thought of Mary Beth until tonight. Having Monica show me how to dress up was like having my childhood friend return to me.

Though it was only a whisper of sound, I heard the bedroom door open. I could see a square of light floating towards me. Someone was using their smartphone as a flashlight.

Irrationally, I felt guilty for thinking about Mary Beth and instead of confronting whoever was there, I closed my eyes and pretended to be asleep. Whoever it was walked softly. I couldn't tell how close he or she was until I heard him breathing above me. The body odor was manly, but pleasant. I recognized it. My late night visitor was Rodney.

He gently lifted the bedsheets. I wondered if he was going to climb into bed with me. I wondered how I would react if he did. My skin prickled in anticipation.

Instead, he lowered the sheet and soon I heard the bedroom door close. I took a deep breath. As if the memory of Mary Beth's princess party wasn't confusing enough, I was now bothered by the fact that I knew Rodney's scent.

CHAPTER FOURTEEN
THREE TIMES A LADY

I spent the next week in taking a crash course in crossdressing. Monica showed me how to talk, walk, and sit like a woman. No more manspreading. The walking turned out to be the hardest part. I kept swishing my hips too extravagantly. Monica said it made me look like I was doing a parody of a streetwalker. The solution turned out to be high heels. Once I had gotten past the wobbling and was able to walk with a small degree of confidence, I found it easier to maneuver in heels if I moved my hips from side to side. Monica said the heels made my ass look great, which bothered me at first but then I accepted it as a compliment.

Jerrica and I still worked out in the gym every day only now I wore women's workout clothes. Jerrica insisted that I wear a sports bra with silicone inserts so that I could get used to the extra weight on my chest when I dressed up.

I went from the small butt plug to the medium butt plug with no problems, but when we got to the biggest one, I balked.

"There is no way that snake is going to fit in my ass," I insisted as I held up the large black object.

"You've already had bigger up there," Jerrica said. "I've seen Rodney's dick. This is nothing compared to his anaconda. Now bend over, girl."

I used to hate it when she called me girl, but now I was used to it. I bent over the table with my bare butt exposed. I heard the snap of the rubber gloves and the squirt of the lubricant. I felt Jerrica's fingers probe my ass as she lubed me. I felt the pressure of the head of the plug as she nudged it into me. I bit my lower lip in anticipation of the agony to come.

But the pain never came. I felt pressure inside me, but it wasn't painful. In fact, it felt…nice.

"Tell me when it's all the way in," I said.

"Oh, we already past all the way in," Jerrica said. "How does it feel?"

"Okay."

"How about when I do this?"

The nice feeling escalated to very nice. I could feel the familiar stirring in my balls. I was started to get an erection. I wanted more.

"What are you doing?" I gasped.

"I'm rotating it. And pushing it in and out. Girl, you are just about ready for the real thing. Now wear this one for the rest of the day. And don't play with it."

Once Monica was convinced I had learned how to act like a lady, she wanted to teach me how to act like a whore. She held the realistic looking black dick dildo in one hand. The loving way she stroked it with her other hand made me think that two of them wanted to be alone.

"First of all, I'll show you how to go down on your man without choking," she said. "And second, I'll show you how to give your man the most amazing blowjob of his life."

"First of all," I said, "I wish you wouldn't refer to Rodney as 'my man.' And second, why would I want to be good at giving head when I don't even want to a dick in my mouth to begin with?"

Monica rolled her eyes. She did that a lot with me.

"The better the blowjob, the quicker he'll come."

"Okay, show me what to do."

Monica gave a demonstration and then she had me try it. I ended up gagging and coming close to vomiting. Monica explained again and I had the same result.

"You're going at it too fast," she said. "Take your time. Enjoy it."

"How am I supposed to do that?"

I expected Monica to roll her eyes again, but instead she smiled and stroked my face.

"Don't you enjoy giving Raegan pleasure when you make love to her?" she asked.

"Sure. I love making her feel good."

"What about before you were married? Did you have the same attitude toward the women you slept with?"

"Yes. I did. I like to think I was a very considerate lover."

"Now stop thinking male and female. Start thinking people giving people pleasure with whatever equipment they happen to have."

I held the base of the rubber dildo. It flopped from side to side.

"This isn't exactly people."

"You have a point. Well, if I'm going to be a good teacher, then I'll just have to make sacrifices. Come on, let's go to your bedroom."

Once we were in the bedroom, Monica began to unbutton her blouse.

"What are you doing?" I asked.

"Giving you a real live dick to practice on," she replied. "This will be easier if you're naked as well."

As we stripped off our clothes, I felt mixed feelings. When I first laid eyes on Monica, I had wondered what she would look like naked, but that was before I found out that she was a chick with a dick. She had a beautiful body with great tits, a flat stomach, and smooth shapely legs.

When she took off her panties, I was shocked at the size of her cock. It was bigger than mine. Where the hell had she been hiding that thing?

Monica lay on the bed on her back, her head resting on a pile of pillows. She patted the space next to her. I stretched out beside her and looked at her cock. I don't normally think about other guy's dicks, but she had a great looking dick. It curved slightly to the left. Like me, her pubic hair was completely shaved off and the skin around her dick was smooth.

"You can touch it," she said. "It won't bite."

I reached over and gently held her cock in my hand, marveling at its texture and warmth. This wasn't at all like holding my own.

"Now, just give it a hello lick," Monica said.

I did as she instructed. Her dick didn't have the heavy funky smell of Rodney and his ex-NBA buddies. Monica's dick was clean and lightly perfumed. It was like licking a pussy that just happened to be a dick. As I ran my tongue the length of her shaft, her dick grew harder and she breathed in quickly.

"Turn your head to the side before putting my dick in your mouth," she said. "It will be easier on your throat."

I did as she instructed. More mixed feelings rushed through me. I was glad I wasn't choking, but I also liked the taste. I wasn't supposed to like the taste of dick.

Monica gave me pointers as I slowly gave her head. When something felt good, she would sigh and praise me. I looked forward to that sigh the same way I looked forward to Raegan's sighs when I ate her pussy. Another mixed feeling came when I felt equally proud and ashamed when I successfully deep-throated her dick without gagging.

"You're doing wonderful, Cole," Monica said. "But here comes the true test. I want you to look at me while you're sucking my dick. I want you to look into my eyes with a look of gratitude, as if nothing in the world makes you happier than blowing my cock and if your mouth wasn't full you would beg me for the chance to swallow my come."

I'm no actor and I'm a lousy liar. Besides, how was I supposed to convey that bullshit with my eyes? But I already had the head of her dick tickling the back of my throat, I might as well try. I looked into her eyes and she winked at me.

I didn't have to act. I did want to make her happy. Monica was right. I had to stop thinking male and female. I was a person giving another person pleasure. I was grateful for all she had done for me. I did want to suck her cock and I desperately wanted her to come in my mouth.

I closed my eyes and made love to her cock with my mouth. I swirled my tongue around the shaft and cupped her balls in my hand. I reached my free hand under her lovely ass and squeezed. I could feel her getting harder. I snaked a finger into her ass and was rewarded with a sigh and an "Oh my God!"

Monica ran her fingers through my long hair. "If you keep that up, I'm going to come," she said.

I could tell she was about to come from the way her cock throbbed. I decided to see how much I could control her orgasm with my mouth. I pulled back and squeezed the base of her cock. The throbbing stopped, but her cock got harder.

"Oh shit," Monica said. "We didn't go over this part. You figured it out on your own. Face it, Cole. You're just like me. You were born to suck cock."

I brought her to the edge again before pulling back. I looked up into her eyes. She was sweating and had a dazed look on her face. She mouthed a plea to release her.

I closed my eyes and concentrated on her dick. I teased it to the edge again. I dug my finger deeper into her ass. When I felt her close to orgasm again, I opened my eyes and looked into her face.

"I see it," she cried. "You want me to come. How can I say no?"

Monica threw back her head and grabbed her nipples. She squealed as her cock jerked and filled my mouth with her salty come. I kept sucking and swallowing until her cock was limp and even then I didn't want to let it go. She slowly pulled out of my mouth and gave me a long, lingering kiss.

"And now it's your turn," she said.

I'd been concentrating so much on her dick that I didn't even notice that mine was rock hard. Monica pushed she back on the pillows and climbed between my legs. As her open mouth inched closer to my erect dick, I got really excited. Suddenly, I desperately needed to come. She winked as her lips slid over the head and my shaft disappeared into her mouth. She gave me the look of gratitude. I was so excited that I came immediately.

We cuddled under the covers. I held her sweaty body close to mine. I marveled at how nice her breasts felt against my smooth chest. I wondered briefly what it would feel like to have breasts like that and then the thought flitted away.

"I give you an A plus," Monica said. "I think you're ready for the big leagues and when it comes to Rodney, I do mean big."

"How do you know Rodney?" I asked.

"I was the chauffer before Penelope."

"I don't believe you. Something tells me nobody made you who you are today. You were born this way."

Monica giggled. "You're right. I worked hard to be the real me. As for Rodney, we met at a club years ago when he was still trying to figure out who he really was. He was playing for Duke at the time and was getting a lot of attention from NBA scouts. He kept his homosexuality a secret for obvious reasons. He didn't think anyone in a gay club would know who he was, but come on, queers like watching sweaty men with bulging muscles slamming into each other as much as straight people do. I noticed that he liked men smaller than him. He was a classic top."

"So, you're a bottom?" I asked as I pinched her adorable ass.

Monica yelped. "I'm flexible," she said. "It depends on who I'm with. Sometimes I like to dominate and sometimes I like to be dominated. With Rodney, I decided that what he really needed most was a friend. We've been fuck buddies from time to time and I may be the one responsible for turning him on to transgendered women, but our strongest bond has been our friendship. Over the years, I've gotten to know him better than he knows himself. He doesn't realize it, but what he's really looking for is love. But then he screws up any chance of a real relationship by turning the sissies he's hot for into black cock hungry sluts."

I was tired of talking about Rodney. It just reminded me of the hell I was stuck in. We fell asleep holding each other's dick.

"Wake up, sleepy head."

I opened my eyes. We had started the blowjob lesson in the morning and now it was late afternoon. I felt more rested than I had in months. Monica stood at the foot of the bed, dressed and looking fresh and clean.

"When will I see you again?" I asked.

"I'm not leaving yet," she said. "You did so well today that I decided you needed a reward. We're going out tonight. Just you and me."

I sat up in bed and blinked at Monica. "Go out? Like on a date?"

"Yes. I talked to Jerrica about it and she thinks it's a great idea. We agreed that you've been cooped up in here for too long."

I got out of bed and went to the bathroom to pee. As I stood over the bowl, I noticed how rank my breath was. I had blowjob breath! After I was done peeing, I brushed my teeth and gargled with mouthwash.

"This is great," I said. "I just need to get some of my clothes from my old room. God, I've been taking hormone pills for so long, I hope I can pass as a man."

Monica crossed her arms. "Oh no. You're going dressed as a woman. This will be a good test to see how well you've learned your lessons."

My heart sank. "Do I have to? I just want to be my old self for one night. Besides, I don't feel safe going out as a woman. It's one thing to do it inside the mansion. I can't handle doing it in public."

"Don't worry. We're going to a gay bar. Nobody will even notice you."

CHAPTER FIFTEEN
PRACTICE MAKES PERFECT

The electronic dance music's thumping beat vibrated through my body. I couldn't hear a word Monica was saying to me. I leaned in close so she could shout into my ear.

"Stop tugging at your dress!"

Monica had picked out the dress, if you could call it that, I was wearing. It was skintight and barely covered my ass. I kept trying to pull it down lower, but there wasn't enough fabric. To make matters worse, the dress was neon pink so there was no way I could disappear in a crowd. I wouldn't have let Raegan leave the house wearing this thing, yet here I was squeezed into this elastic sausage casing in the middle of this enormous dance club.

Monica had great fun dressing me up for the evening. The dress included a choker that hid my Adam's apple. I wore black spiked heels and carried a tiny purse on a gold chain over my shoulder. I had on tons of eyeliner, fake lashes, fake nails, and fake breasts that were larger than what I normally had to wear. When Monica was finally done, I looked at myself in the mirror and was amazed. I looked like a total slut. But more importantly, I looked more like a woman dressed like a slut than a man dressed as a woman dressed like a slut.

I had to stare deep into my own eyes to find the man hidden inside me. Or maybe I was seeing the woman that had been hidden from me all this time. For a moment, I swayed from the confusion. I reminded myself that I only had a few months to go. Soon, I wouldn't be burdened with these bizarre questions.

Monica had dressed up as well. She wore a blue miniskirt that hugged her curves and brought out the blue in her eyes. She had teased her blonde hair so that it was almost as tall as me. I don't know how she did it, but somehow she didn't look slutty. She just looked ravishing.

Dressing up in the safe confines of the mansion and being exposed out in the real world were two different things. I was terrified and held onto Monica's arm as we made our way through the club. Flashing colored lights from the ceiling lit up the darkness.

We wormed our way to the bar. Monica ordered two Gin and tonics. We took our drinks and stood in the corner to people watch. Many of the women were wearing skimpier outfits than me. I looked like a nun by comparison. Some of the men wore less than the women. The thing the two groups had in common was the evidence that they worked out a lot. But beyond the tight bodies, I noticed many people with regular bodies. Everyone seemed to be having a great time hanging out together. Women were hugging women, men were kissing men, and groups of men and women laughed and danced together.

"Can you tell which of the women were born as men?" Monica asked.

I scanned the women and identified the crossdressers by their larger hands, wigs, scarves around their necks, and bodies that were slightly more masculine than feminine. Seeing them made me feel more at ease.

After a couple more Gin and tonics, Monica talked me into getting on the dance floor with her. We entered the mass of bodies writhing to the pulsing music. I was never much of a dancer and Monica hadn't taught me how to dance like a girl. I mimicked whatever she did. She swung her hips from side to side while doing a simple two step so I swung my hips from side to side while doing a simple two step. I aped the way she moved her hands as if she were brushing her hair aside while having an orgasm. I didn't mimic her duck face. I had my limits.

We worked up a good sweat and went to the bar to cool off with another Gin and tonic. Monica suggested I order the next round. I smiled at the bartender and damned if he didn't hop over to take my order. Being a girl definitely had its advantages. When the drinks arrived, I dug into my tiny purse for the money that Jerrica had put in there for me.

Along with the money, the purse held make-up and lipstick. What I didn't have was an ID, a phone, or keys. Unless I was going into my own backyard or to go jogging, I never left my house without at least taking my driver's license.

I held a twenty out for the bartender, but he waved it away.

"It's already been taken care of," he said. "The gentlemen over there paid for your drinks."

He pointed at two men at the end of the bar. They held their beer bottles up in salute. I'd never tried the tactic of buying a woman a drink, but here I was on the receiving end. I turned to Monica in a blind panic.

"They're trying to pick us up," I said. "What do we do?"

"You silly goose," she said. "Just because they bought us a drink doesn't mean we owe them anything more than polite company and maybe a dance. Come on, this is a good opportunity to practice your female voice."

"I don't think I can pull it off. They're bound to figure out that I'm a man."

"Have you already forgotten where we are? I'm sure they already know."

The two men sauntered over to us. One was black and one was white. They were taller than Monica but shorter than me. My heels added even more height so that they were eye level with my fake breasts. They wore the recent fashion for men that I hadn't embraced yet, suits that seemed two sizes too small.

"Hello ladies," said the white guy. "My name's Derick and this is Anthony."

"Pleased to meet you," Monica said. "I'm Monica and this is Colette."

I glanced at Monica and she winked. I hadn't thought about using a girl's name, but it made sense that I should. We drank our drinks and the men talked about their jobs as commercial insurance inspectors. I had to stifle a laugh because that was my job and from their conversation I could tell from the way they described their work day that they weren't very good inspectors. While we talked, Derick and Anthony blatantly undressed us with their eyes.

"I have to go to the ladies' room," Monica announced. "Come on, Colette."

I always wondered what women did when they went to the bathroom together and after all those Gin and tonics, I had to piss like a racehorse so I followed her eagerly. I hesitated at the door with the restroom symbol for women. The stick figure with the triangle hips meant penises were not allowed. Monica giggled, grabbed my hand, and pulled me inside.

There was a serious lack of urinals. The shortage was covered with more toilet stalls. Women were lined up in front of the mirror, checking their make-up and hair. The air was thick with a combination of urine and perfume.

I ducked into an empty stall, pulled up my dress, pulled down my panties, and lifted the toilet seat. Monica knocked on the stall door.

"Colette," she hissed. "Sit down and pee like a girl.

Shit. Reluctantly, I lowered the seat, sat down *like a girl*, and relieved my bladder. I came out of the stall and Monica was nowhere in sight. Had she left me? But then, I heard the toilet flush in the stall next to the one I'd used and she emerged. She led me to the mirror and pointed out that my make-up and lipstick needed to be refreshed. Now I understood why women spent so much time in the bathroom. There was so much work involved in being a girl.

"So what do you think of Derick and Anthony?" Monica asked.

"They seem like nice guys," I said.

"They're seriously cute. Which one do you want? Considering your preference for dark meat, I'm going to guess Anthony. That's okay. I'll take Derick. You can tell he works out."

"Uh, you can have both of them."

Monica laughed and hugged me. "You should have seen the look of fear on your face. Of course we didn't come here to get laid. But come on, admit it. You're having fun playing the part of the hot chick, aren't you?"

I finished applying lipstick and checked my reflection to make sure I didn't get any on my teeth.

"You're right," I said. "I'm having fun. I know that they know I'm a dude, but I'm still enjoying myself. I thought tonight would be terrible, but I was wrong. Thank you for forcing me to do this."

"I didn't have to twist your arm to get you out tonight. I told you before that this might be the real you."

I looked at myself more closely in the mirror. An attractive woman stared back at me. I felt a warm feeling in my stomach. Was this really the real me or was I just enjoying playing a part? Was I just exploring my sexuality and trying on a different persona for kicks?

Tonight had been exhilarating, scary, and weird. It was as close to an out of body experience as I ever had. I didn't want to overanalyze it. That brought in too many frightening questions. I was just going to enjoy this night for what it was.

"When I was in college, some of my fraternity brothers thought if they bought a girl a few drinks, that she owed them sex," I said. "What do I do if Derick or Anthony puts a move on me?"

"Do you want to fuck them?" Monica asked.

"What? No! But I don't want to have to punch them in the face either."

"You don't have to do anything you don't want to do. We don't owe them anything. We hung out with them. That's more than enough payment. As for me, if Derick tried to kiss me, I would let him, but if he tried to feel me up, I would calmly move his hands off my body and walk away. If that didn't work, then I'd punch him in the face. I've done it before."

I was relieved. I wasn't sure why I was worried in the first place.

"However," Monica continued. "If Derick or Anthony puts a move on you, I want you to go let him. There's a room in the back that's kept dark where people can have sex. If he takes you back there, I want you to give him the best blowjob of his young life."

I felt the blood rush from my face. I tugged at my dress nervously.

"But you just said, I didn't have to do anything I didn't want to do," I said.

"Yeah, but you need the practice. You gave me a great blowjob this afternoon. Show one of those lucky boys what you learned."

"No," I said defiantly.

Monica put her arms around me and pulled me close to her. Her teased blonde hair tickled my chin.

"Come on, Colette," she cooed. "You know deep down you're dying to get one of those hot boy's cock in your warm mouth. You can't wait to control him with your tongue and to make him moan with ecstasy as his come slides down your throat."

"That's not true," I said weakly.

"Then why can I feel your erection against my stomach?"

I stepped back and looked down. The tight material of my dress made my boner clearly visible. An attractive woman with a mountain of hair glanced at my bulge and shook her head.

"Honey," she said. "You got to tuck that thing in tight before you go out."

"Considering all the estrogen you've been taking, I'm surprised you're getting this many erections," Monica said.

I sighed and tried to place my tiny purse over the bulge.

"Okay, I'll do the blowjob," I said. "But only if one of the guys puts the move on me. Which probably won't even happen."

"Don't be so sure of that."

We waited until my erection died down before leaving the ladies' room. Anthony was waiting for us.

"We got a table and a fresh round of drinks," he announced. "Come on. Follow me."

He led us through the crowd to a half circle booth. Derick was seated in the middle and smiled when he saw us. Monica and I slid in followed by Anthony. Though there was plenty of space left on the booth, Anthony scooted in so close to me that our legs were touching. I took a sip of my drink to calm my nerves.

"What do you say we take some Molly?" Derick said. He opened the palm of his hand to reveal four capsules filled with white powder.

"I don't know," I said. "I heard this shit's dangerous."

Derick chuckled. "Anything worth doing is a little dangerous. I've taken it dozens of times and haven't had any problems."

I looked at Monica. "What do you think?"

She took one of the capsules from Derick's palm and popped it into her mouth. I shrugged, grabbed one, and swallowed it. Derick and Anthony took the last two. For the first ten minutes, I didn't notice anything, but then I began to relax and felt really good. I can't remember our conversation, but I started laughing because everything they said seemed really funny. Anthony put his hand on my leg and it didn't bother me at all. In fact, I liked it and put my hand on his leg.

"Hey, Colette," Anthony said.

"What?" I asked.

"Lean in close to me. There's something I want to tell you."

I leaned close to his face and he kissed me on the lips. His tongue snaked into my mouth. I kissed him back. I liked it. I wanted to kiss him so more, but he pulled back. My cheeks were flushed. I was full of energy.

"I want to dance," I said. "Dance with me."

"Sure," Anthony said.

I grabbed Monica's arm. "Anthony and I are going to dance."

"Have fun," Monica said and then she turned back to Derick as he put his arm around her.

Anthony and I got on the dance floor. Whatever inhibitions I had before about dancing in a dress out in public had vanished. My body swayed to the beat as if it were the most natural thing in the world. Anthony was so handsome. Why hadn't I noticed that before? His caramel colored skin looked delicious. Everything about him was delicious.

He put his hand around my waist and pulled me close to him. I put my arms around his broad shoulders. We looked into each other's eyes. Heat was practically rising off of us like steam. He spun me around and grinded his groin against my ass.

I was enjoying dancing, but I also really wanted to suck Anthony's dick. Maybe it was the Molly or maybe this was the real me. Maybe I'd always been bisexual or maybe I was really a girl inside. It didn't matter. Dancing with Anthony had turned me on so much that all I could think about was how soon I could get his erection poking the back of my throat.

I turned to face him and pulled him close to me.

"Take me to the dark room," I said. "Take me now."

Anthony grinned from ear to ear. He took my hand and led me to the back of the club, down a flight of stairs, and along a long hallway to a red door. He knocked twice. A man in a black T-shirt and black jeans opened the door. He looked me over and smirked. He held the door open while Anthony pulled me inside.

I couldn't see a thing. The room was pitch black. I could hear moans and groans. The funky scent of sex was overpowering. As my eyes adjusted, I could see that there was some light. Blue lightbulbs gave off a minimum amount of illumination and turned everyone in the room blue.

There were no chairs so everyone was either standing or squatting. The room was about the size of a basketball half court. Anthony and I moved about cautiously; we didn't want to bump into anybody while they were busy getting laid.

By the time we located an open area next to the wall, I could see more clearly. It was like a Smurf orgy. Blue people were screwing each other in every way possible. Men had their pants down around their ankles and women had their dresses hiked up over their hips, but then again, I couldn't tell if the people dressed as men were male or if the people dressed as women were female. Some people had stripped completely naked. Mostly it was couples coupling, but there were groups of threes and fours as well.

Anthony pressed me against the wall and kissed me. His tongue worked its way into my mouth again. I could taste the Gin he'd been drinking. I reached down and massaged the front of his pants. I could feel the bulge of his cock. Anthony nuzzled my neck as he grinded his groin against mine. His hands reached around and grabbed my ass. I wished I had tits so he could suck my nipples.

I fumbled with his belt and undid his pants. I reached inside his boxer shorts and my hand grasped his cock. It was warm and smooth. As I kneeled down, I pulled his cock out. It wasn't as big as Rodney's, but it was plenty big. I licked a drop of pre-come off the tip and savored the salty sperm.

It was too dark to look into his eyes, so I concentrated on pleasuring him with my mouth. I jerked on his tool until it was rigid and then I wrapped my mouth around the head. Anthony moaned as I went down on his cock. I held onto the base of his shaft as I sucked, but he pushed my hand away.

"Don't use your hands," he barked. "Just your mouth."

His bossy and arrogant attitude was more of a turn on than I expected. Since my desire was to please him, I liked that he had taken charge. I kept my hands away as I sucked his cock.

"Play with my balls."

I cupped his heavy balls in my hand as I continued to slide my mouth up and down his shaft.

"Hold still."

I stopped moving. His cock rested inside my mouth. His heavy musk filled my nostrils. His rough pubic hair tickled my face. He grabbed my head and fucked my face furiously. I did my best not to choke as he rammed his cock down my throat again and again. A trickle of saliva dribbled out of my mouth and hung off my chin.

He was getting close. But then, he pulled out. I couldn't help whimpering in frustration. I was so looking forward to his hot come filling my waiting mouth.

"Stand up and face the wall."

I stood and turned toward the wall. He ran his hands over my ass, squeezing each cheek.

"Pull up your dress. Slowly."

It was just supposed to be a blowjob. I hadn't planned on getting fucked. I silently thanked Jerrica for making me work my way up from the smallest to the biggest butt plug.

I slowly pulled my tight dress up and uncovered my panties. My erect dick strained against the silk fabric.

"Now slowly pull down your panties."

My legs shook as I inched my panties down. As soon as I got them past my dick, it popped out and hung in the air. I felt like the whole room was watching me exposing myself.

"How far do you want me to pull the down?" I asked.

"Take them off. Give them to me. I'll make sure you don't lose them."

I worked them over my heels and held them in my hand. I didn't turn to face Anthony. He snatched the panties out of my hand. I could hear him breathe in deeply. He was sniffing my panties.

"Bend over and put your hands on the wall. Then spread your legs."

I did as he instructed. I felt like I was about to be frisked by the police. I waited for what seemed like an eternity and then Anthony stuck his tongue in my ass crack.

His tongue darted in and out of my asshole. My balls tingled and my dick ached for relief. When he stuck a finger inside my ass, I almost came. He probed me with one finger, then two, and then three. What was he waiting for? Why didn't he fuck me already?

Finally, the head of his cock nudged against my asshole. It felt different from when Rodney and his friends entered my ass and I realized it was because Anthony was wearing a condom. I would have thanked him for practicing safe sex, but I didn't want to slow him down.

Though his cock entered my ass easily, it felt like a baseball bat had been shoved all the way to my stomach.

"Damn, your ass is tight. I love a good tight ass."

He grabbed my hips and fucked me hard.
"Open that pussy for me."

I grabbed my ass cheeks and pulled them out. His cock rammed into my widened hole. He grunted each time he thrust his hips forward and I moaned as I lifted my ass to meet his cock. My mind was consumed with the building lust inside me.

"Do you like my cock?" he asked.

"I love your cock," I said.

"Do you want me to come in your ass?"

"Yes."

"Then ask me to come in your ass."

"Please come in my ass. Please come in my ass. I love your cock so much."

He held still and his cock jerked. His sperm filled my ass and slithered down my leg. My cock jerked too and my come splattered against the wall. I couldn't believe it. I had come without touching my cock. I'd had an anal orgasm. My ass really was my pussy.

We stayed connected until his limp cock slid out of my ass. Anthony pulled up his boxer shorts and pants. I pulled my dress down. Anthony clutched my panties in his hand, but when I reached out for them, he held them away from me.

"Very funny," I said. "Now give me my panties back. I can't leave the club without them."

"First give me a kiss," he said.

I pulled him to me and gave him a long lingering kiss. He held me close to him as we made out.

"Now will you give me my panties back?" I asked when we finally came up for air.

"No," he said firmly. "You have to go around the rest of tonight without them. Then, you have to come home with me and let my roommates fuck you and come on your face. And then maybe, just maybe I'll give you your panties back."

My head was still spinning from the sex and the Molly so I was having a hard time concentrating. What he was insisting I do was dangerous and scary, but part of me wanted to go with him and do whatever nasty thing he told me to do.

"I don't know," I muttered. "I can't think straight. I think I want to go home."

"Come on. You're nothing but a little whore. Stop misbehaving or I'll have to punish you."

That part about punishing me blew away a good portion of the haze in my head. I was in trouble and I needed to get away from this guy. He could keep the panties as a souvenir.

I started to walk away, but he grabbed my arm and pulled me back. He raised his hand as if to slap me. I clenched my fists, as if to punch him in the balls.

"I wouldn't do that if I were you."

We turned to see who was talking. It was Monica. She and Derick stood behind us. Monica had her arms crossed.

"Hey, this is between me and Colette," Anthony said.

"Give the lady her panties back, thank you for a wonderful evening, and walk the fuck away," Monica said firmly.

Anthony moved toward Monica, but Derick got between them and put his hands on Anthony's shoulders.

"Do as she says," Derrick said. "Monica has a lot of connections. She can get you banned from all the clubs. Give Colette her panties back and let's scoot."

Anthony stared at the floor for a minute and then he gave my panties a final sniff before handing them over to me.

"I had a wonderful evening," he said. "Let's do it again sometime."

I didn't say anything. He and Derick left the dark room. Once they were gone, I quickly put my panties back on. I was embarrassed, like the teacher had caught me breaking the rules. Monica and I went to the ladies' room so I could clean up.

My make-up was a mess. As I reapplied my mascara and lipstick, Monica smirked.

"I know," I said. "I let the situation get out of hand. I should have known better."

"Honey, you were fine," Monica said. "Anthony just turned out to be a jerk. A true dominant doesn't force a submissive to do anything they haven't consented to."

"Is that what I am? A submissive?"

"Tonight you were. Don't give it too much thought. Molly can make you do things you don't normally do."

"How come you didn't get as fucked up as I did?"

Monica opened her purse and took out a white capsule.

"I didn't take the Molly," she said. "I only pretended to. I wanted to keep an eye on you in case you got into trouble, especially since this was your first time taking the drug."

"It's a good thing you did." I finished doing my face. "How do I look?"

"Perfect. You've learned how to do it all by yourself. My little girl is all grown up."

I smiled at Monica. "Your little girl wants to go home."

CHAPTER SIXTEEN
CROSSING THE LINE

I woke up with a pounding headache. I stumbled out of bed determined to go to my workout with Jerrica regardless of the agony. The room spun and I quickly laid back down. The phone on my nightstand rang. The shrill sound rattled my brain and I snatched the receiver to shut it up.

"Hullo?" I mumbled.

"Heard you had a big night," Jerrica said much too cheerfully.

"Yeah."

"How does your head feel?"

"Like it's going to explode."

"I have a home remedy that works like a charm. I'll have one of the maids bring it up to you. You can skip the workout for today."

"Bless you."

"Besides, you need your rest."

I immediately became suspicious.

"Oh yeah? Why do I need my rest?"

"Because you're going on a date tonight."

"Tonight?"

"Rodney wants to have dinner alone with you."

"Where?"

"Here in the mansion. Don't worry. It'll be very laid back."

"Hey, I'm working for him. If he wants to have a laid back dinner with me, I'll be there."

"Don't forget to give yourself an enema. He wants your asshole nice and clean."

Jerrica hung up before I could ask any more questions. My head hurt too much to think about it and I went back to bed. I was almost back to sleep when a maid came in the room. It was Susie, Jerrica's girlfriend. She carried a small silver tray and on it was a glass filled with a green liquid.

"What the hell is this shit?" I asked.

"Don't ask," she said. "Just drink it fast."

I downed the vile looking concoction. I expected to vomit it out seconds later, but instead it settled my stomach and the throbbing in my head slowed down to a dull ache.

"Should I bring up some breakfast?" Susie asked. "Or would you rather catch up on your beauty sleep?"

I gave her the stink eye. "Sleep," I said.

I pulled the covers over my head and fell asleep. I didn't even hear Susie leave the room.

When I woke up, I checked the time. I'd been in a deep, dreamless sleep for six hours. Whatever Jerrica put in that green drink should be patented because my headache was gone and I felt great.

I put on my workout clothes and went to the gym. Jerrica had gotten me so used to daily exercising that I didn't feel right if I missed a day. I was still recuperating from my wild night at the club so I didn't overdo it. I managed to sweat out some of the toxins I'd ingested.

I went back to my room and took a long hot shower. Entering the bedroom from a cloud of steam, I smelled coffee. Susie stood next to a rolling tray. She took a cover off a plate to reveal an egg white omelet and dry toast. My stomach grumbled. I hadn't eaten since the night before. But more important than the food was the coffee. I poured a cup and sipped it gratefully.

"All this pampering is starting to worry me," I said.

"This is nothing," Susie said. "There's a whole parade of people coming here today to pamper you. Rodney wants you to feel like a princess today."

"The last time Rodney was this nice to me, he and his NBA buddies gang raped me."

Susie looked around as if to make sure nobody could hear us. We were alone in the bedroom, so unless the room was bugged and I wouldn't have been surprised if it had been, there was no one around but the two of us.

"Rodney is one of those guys who has a tendency to kill a fly with a sledgehammer," Susie said. "That night with his NBA buddies was a mistake. Jerrica told him so."

"Is this his way of saying he's sorry?"

"I can't always read Rodney. I just know that he really likes you and he's going overboard to show you how he feels. If I were you, I'd just enjoy the ride."

I thought about Jerrica's instruction that I give myself an enema. I wondered just what kind of ride Susie was referring to.

Susie wasn't kidding about a parade of people coming to pamper me. I barely had time to finish breakfast before they started arriving. My body hair had begun to grow back, so May and Jing came and made my legs, ass, and face smooth and hairless again. "No sex this time," May said. "Strictly business," Jing added. Kenny, the heavily tattooed stylist, did my hair. His hair was no longer purple. Now it was green. After snipping away at my mane for thirty minutes, I somehow managed to look like I had longer and fuller hair than before. A round Mexican woman I'd never seen before waddled in and gave me a manicure and a pedicure. When she left, my nails and toenails were painted a deep red.

Throughout the whole afternoon, Susie had stuck close by, ushering people in and out, and making sure I stayed hydrated. When the Mexican woman left, whose name I learned was Maria, Susie suggested I take a short nap. I agreed. I was exhausted.

Susie woke me up three hours later. I hadn't intended to sleep that long. The sun was starting to go down. I excused myself and went to the bathroom. I gave myself an enema and then took a shower. When I came out, matching black bra and panties were laid out on the bed and a pair of black open toed high heels waited on the floor. Susie stood next to the bed holding a clothing bag.

"What's all this?" I asked.

"Rodney picked out your clothes for tonight, all the way down to the underwear."

"What a control freak."

"Wait until you see the dress he picked out."

My cheeks burned with anger. I was sure that damn French maid's outfit was inside the clothing bag Susie was holding.

"Oh no! There is no way I'm wearing that fucking dress. He's taken that joke way too far."

Susie opened to clothing bag to reveal an elegant red evening gown. Susie explained that it was a sleeveless key hole beaded waist Jersey dress. All I knew was that it was beautiful. After I got dressed, I looked at myself in the mirror. The hormone treatments had given me soft womanly curves and the dress made me appear like a princess on her way to the prince's ball.

I could understand if Rodney had had me dress up as a sexy slut, but this was extremely romantic. It shook me to my core.

Susie did my make-up, picked out a nice perfume for me, and brushed out my hair. When she was done, I checked myself in the mirror again. I was absolutely gorgeous and I smelled amazing. Cole had disappeared and Colette had taken his place.

For her last chore of the evening, Susie led me through the crazy maze of the mansion to a back patio that I'd never seen before and I'd been here for months. The weather was just starting to feel like Fall was on its way so it was a perfect night to eat outdoors. There were vases of flowers set up everywhere so the air was sweet with their combined scent. Strings of lights lit up the patio.

Rodney was seated at a table for two and stood when he saw me. He was dressed in a very expensive looking tailored suit. As I approached him, he smiled and held up his hand.

"Wait," he said. "Let me drink this in." He rubbed his chin as he checked me out. "Turn around. I want to see the whole package." I spun around and the dress flared out and flowed around my legs. "Girl, you really clean up good."

"You clean up pretty good yourself," I said.

I looked back so I could thank Susie for everything she'd done for me today, but she had already taken off. It was just Rodney and me. He held my chair out for me. I hesitated. This was new territory for me, but I sat down and let him scoot me toward the table.

"I heard that you used the name Colette last night," Rodney said. "Do you mind if I call you Colette?"

"You're buying me dinner; you can call me whatever you like."

Dinner was already on the table under covered dishes. A bottle of champagne was cooling in a bucket of ice. I don't remember what we ate, just that it was delicious and the champagne was excellent. It was the conversation that stuck with me. Rodney asked me about myself and seemed genuinely interested in getting to know me. I was curious about him and peppered him with questions.

After dinner and two more bottles of champagne, we moved on from personal information to talking sports, books, and our favorite movies. We had much more in common than I ever would have imagined. If we had met in other circumstances, we might have been buddies.

"Let's take a walk," Rodney said.

A walk sounded good. We'd been sitting for long time and I wanted to stretch my legs. Rodney held out his arm. Again I hesitated. This was too much like a romantic date. I reminded myself that this was essentially my job, so I took his arm and let him lead me out onto the rolling lawn that seemed to go on forever. As we walked, I noticed that he wore a nice cologne, but didn't overdo it like most guys.

It was a clear night and the sky was full of stars. The mansion seemed like it was miles away and we were alone on a green island. Rodney slipped his arm around my waist and held me against his side.

"I get lonely sometimes," he said.

I had no response for that.

He scooped his arms around me and kissed me. Without thinking, I wrapped my arms around his neck. When we parted, he looked deep into my eyes.

"I'm going to have sex with you tonight," he said.

"Yes, I know you are."

"Please let me continue. I'm going to have sex with you tonight. You don't have a choice about it. I also want to take control of you and you do have a choice about that. I will ask you to do things for me. I will only do them if you give me permission. If I ask you to do something you're not comfortable doing, then say so and I won't do it. Do you understand?"

"I think I do."

"Good. Let's go to my bedroom."

We walked back to the mansion. The dinner dishes and empty champagne bottles on the patio had already been cleared away. There were people everywhere, but they were invisible.

I had never been to Rodney's bedroom before. I didn't even realize that it was on the same floor as my bedroom. It took us forever to get to it through winding hallways.

The lighting was low and his cologne hung in the air. I was impressed by the complete lack of basketball items. There was no evidence that he was a basketball star. The room was dominated by a California king bed with satin sheets.

Rodney began to undress. He didn't throw his clothes on the floor, but hung his clothes on hangers.

"I want you to strip down to just your panties," Rodney said. He pointed at straight back chair next to a writing desk. "You can put your clothes on that chair."

I did as he instructed. I was a bit embarrassed about how much I hated taking off the beautiful gown. Soon, I only had on the black silk panties Rodney had chosen for me to wear tonight and my high heel shoes. He had stripped down naked.

He had a magnificent body. Power radiated off of him. His muscles were well-defined on his tall frame. I envied his six pack abs. His massive black cock dangled between his legs. My mouth watered in anticipation of feeling it slide down my throat.

"Get on the bed on your hands and knees," Rodney said. "But first, take off your shoes."

I slipped off my shoes and climbed onto the bed. Rodney walked from one side of the bed to the other, examining me. I caught of his cock as he passed within view. It was starting to get hard and bobbed in the air. He slid his hand down my back to my ass and then smacked my ass with the palm of his hand. Shivers rippled through me.

"Arch your back," he said. "Push your pussy out."

I arched my back. Rodney massaged my ass and then his hand slipped down and massaged my dick. I started to get hard. He went back to massaging my ass. As his hand kneaded my cheeks, he kissed me. His tongue darted inside my mouth.

"Are you going to please my cock?" he asked.

"Yes," I replied.

"Speak up, what are you going to do?"

"I'm going to please your cock."

He reached down between my legs and rubbed my cock again. The silk fabric covering my now full erection caused an electric reaction through my loins. He kisses me again with his open mouth. He kisses me with passion and I return the feeling.

Just like the night before with Anthony, I enjoyed having a strong man take control of me. We were playing a game where I didn't have to guess what to do next. Rodney made the decisions for me. And as Rodney said, I could quit playing at any time.

I considered quitting right then because I could. I would thank him for a lovely evening and asked for directions back to my room. But my dick was hard and I was curious to what he would tell me to do next.

Rodney moved away, leaving me on all fours like a dog waiting for his master to tell her which trick to perform. He went to his dresser and took something out of the top drawer. He came back holding a plastic bottle in one hand and a syringe in the other. That syringe frightened me. He saw the worried look on my face and chuckled.

"Don't worry," he said. "This is just for squirting lube into your ass. Did you think I was going to shoot you up with heroin?"

"I didn't know what to think," I said.

"Take your panties off."

I took my panties off and left them on the edge of the bed.

"Push out your pussy."

It still felt odd to have my ass referred to as a vagina, but since he was going to fuck my ass, I suppose it was my vagina. I arched my back.

Rodney inserted the syringe into my ass and I felt it fill with lube. He pulled out the syringe and smacked my ass. He probed me with his large finger. My ass opened up to him. He squirted some lube on his fingers and slathered it on my dick. He stroked my dick and it felt so wonderful that I almost came right then and there.

"If you suck cock like I tell you to, then you'll get laid," Rodney said. "Do you want to suck my cock?"

"Yes," I replied.

"Do you really want to suck my cock or are you saying it because you think that's what I want to hear?"

"Both."

Rodney chuckled. "An honest answer. I like that."

He sat down on the bed next to me. His erect cock laid against his left upper thigh.

"Ready to suck cock?"

"Yes."

I leaned down with my open mouth. The head was inches from my lips when Rodney stopped me.

"Lay down so I can play with your ass while you're sucking my cock."

I did as he instructed. I lay on the bed beside him and grabbed the shaft. Again, I was inches away from going down on him when he stopped me again.

"Get your hands off my shaft."

I moved my hand away.

"Cup my balls and open your mouth wide. Make sure you don't touch my cock with your teeth."

After all this starting and stopping, I desperately wanted his cock inside my mouth.

"Now suck my cock."

I cupped his heavy balls in my hand and got as much of his big black cock into my wide open mouth as I could handle. I managed to get halfway down. He just had too much cock to get it all inside my mouth. To compensate, I stroked his shaft.

"What did I just say about touching my shaft," he said sharply. "Just play with my balls. And go deeper."

I lowered my hand back down to his balls. They were delightfully squishy and hairy. I turned my head to the side so I could swallow more of his cock.

"Deeper," he barked.

I breathed through my nose as I struggled to get more of him into my mouth. The head was poking the back of my throat. To keep from choking, I went up and down on his shaft. My saliva dripped down to his balls and I massaged my spit on his skin. His manly smell filled my head, enticing me to go faster.

"Slow down," Rodney said. "There's no time limit. You've got plenty of time to suck my cock."

I slowed my rhythm which made the blowjob more sensuous as I tickled his shaft with my tongue and concentrated on every bump and vein. Going slower made me fall in love with his cock and the maybe the man attached to it.

"Good girl. You're really sucking that cock."

His praise made me proud. I was learning to be a good cocksucker.

"Let me taste some of that cock."

I lifted up and he kissed me with his open mouth as I shared his cock juices with him.

"Get your mouth back on my cock. Go deeper."

I went back down on him and somehow I managed to get his monster cock all the way into my mouth. His rough pubic hair tickled my nose. He placed his hands on top of my head and thrust his cock into my throat. I relaxed my throat and got past my gag reflex. My mouth was also a pussy for his wonderful cock.

I could feel his cock stiffen as he neared orgasm. I didn't want him to come yet. Neither did he. As Rodney pulled his out of my mouth, a string of saliva hung from my lips to the tip of his cock.

Rodney moved so that he was lying fully on the bed with his head on the pillows. He took the bottle of lube from the nightstand where he'd left it and squirted a stream on his cock. He opened his legs wide.

"Rub that in," he said.

I kneeled between his legs and stroked his shaft and rubbed the sticky liquid over the head. He closed his eyes and smiled.

"That's nice. Hold out your hand."

He squirted some of the liquid into the palm of my hand.

"Rub that on your dick and ass."

I lubed my dick and my ass. Both were soon nice and slippery.

"Straddle my cock."

Up until now, men poked their cocks into me. Rodney was telling me to put it in myself. Something about that deliberate act made it clear that I was a willing partner in this sex act. I had been worried for weeks that I would cross a line that I could never return from. Was this the line? Was this the moment when I told Rodney I couldn't go any further?

But I couldn't say no, because I had to find out. Otherwise, I would always wonder if I wanted this, if this was the real me.

I climbed onto Rodney and straddled his hips. His erection rubbed against my ass crack. I grasped it tightly and it writhed in my hands. I steered the head to my asshole. I took a deep breath and relaxed my ass as I pushed Rodney's cock inside. I slid down so that more and more of the shaft inched into me until I was sitting against his groin.

I paused to enjoy how filled up I felt. I swear his cock went all the way to my bellybutton. I slowly humped up and down. Each stroke sent erotic thrills through my body. My toes curled. There was an unfamiliar sound in the room and I realized it was me moaning with pleasure.

"Play with your dick while you're fucking," Rodney said.

I grabbed my dick and stroked it in rhythm to our fucking. This was better than any time before. I could see why guys fucked each other. This was incredible. The smell of our combined musk filled the room.

Rodney grabbed my ass and pulled the cheeks wider so that he could slide in and out easier. Every time I get close to coming, I squeezed the base of my shaft. I wanted to enjoy this for as long as possible. And I didn't want to come before Rodney. If possible, I wanted us to come at the same time.

"Get off," Rodney said. He chuckled at my hurt expression. "Don't worry, girl. We ain't done by a long shot. I'm just changing positon."

I got off Rodney's cock. He had me get on my hands and knees. He placed pillows under my stomach so that I could lean down and thrust my ass in the air. He pushed my legs apart. My head was buried in the pillows as I waited for him to enter me. I didn't have to wait long. He had already opened up my ass and his cock slid in easily.

Apparently, the time for going slow was over. Rodney grabbed my hips and slammed into my ass like a jackhammer. I emitted little moans in time with his thrusts. His balls bounced against mine. I reached between my legs and pumped my dick furiously. I was getting closer to the line of no return, but I wasn't there yet. Maybe I wasn't meant to. Maybe this was fun and games, but not the real me after all.

"Your ass is so fine," Rodney said. "You're the best fuck I've had in ages."

"Thank you," I mumbled into the pillows.

He pulled out of me again. I couldn't take getting so close without relief too many more times. I decided that I wouldn't worry about when I came. I would just let it happen and not worry about when he came.

"Get on your back."

I am covered in sweat. I am consumed with lust. I wanted to come in the worst way, but I almost called it off again. Rodney wanted to fuck me in the missionary position, the classic male on female lovemaking position.

It was too much. I was about to tell him no when he kissed me. His lips pressed against mine and I felt electricity. I lay on my back. He pushed my legs far apart and led his cock to my ass. He kissed me again as he entered me. I could feel his cock deep inside me. I could feel him deep inside me.

He leaned his body against mine as he fucked me in a steady rhythm that wasn't too fast or too slow. He continued to kiss me. Without thinking, I wrapped my arms around his shoulders and my legs around his torso. He slid his arms under me and held me close to him. Our chests were plastered together. My dick rubbed his stomach.

Rodney fucked me like I was his girlfriend. I was his girlfriend. I wanted him to come inside me. I wanted him. I moaned like a little bitch. I chased his cock every time it threatened to escape my pussy ass. I licked the sweat off his neck. He squeezed me against him as he humped me with a fierce desperation.

We came at the same time. He groaned loudly as his hot sperm filled my ass. I moaned as my come coated his stomach. And in that moment, the line was crossed. I knew I would never get enough of black cock, his black cock. This was the real me. I was a black cock hungry white sissy.

As our orgasms subsided, we untangled our bodies and Rodney climbed off of me. I lay on my back and stared at the ceiling. My body was slick with sweat. Rodney's sperm leaked out of my ass and onto his nice sheets. He went to get towels and cool water to drink. He kissed me lightly on the lips before he left.

While I was alone, I wondered how I would go forward with my life? Would I crave black cock from now on? Would I swear off pussy forever? But like any addict, I believed that I could kick the habit at any time. I had less than two months to go before I would return to my old life. And despite my desire for Rodney's big black cock, I was determined to return to that life. In the meantime, I was going to spend these last weeks getting as much of his cock as I could.

CHAPTER SEVENTEEN
PENELOPE RETURNS

After our romantic date, I spent every night in Rodney's bed. We screwed constantly. I couldn't get enough of his big black cock and he couldn't get enough of my sweet white ass. We were a match made in heaven. We also spent a lot of time sucking each other's dicks. I hadn't been this sore from sex since my honeymoon.

As if the marathon fucking wasn't enough, Rodney had great fun thinking of kinky things for me to do. As always, I could have said no, but I was having too much fun pleasing him and his requests never included anything rough or painful.

My favorite was when he invited Marcellus Underwood over for a threesome. Marcellus had no idea that's what was in store for the evening. He thought he and Rodney were going to watch TV and drink beer. But then, Rodney had me come in wearing a garter belt, black stockings, spiked high heels, a leather choker, and nothing else. Marcellus claimed he almost came in his pants when he saw me. I ended up on my hands and knees sucking Marcellus' cock while Rodney fucked my ass. And then the two men changed positions. After a few sweaty hours of this, they both ejaculated on my face at the same time.

I found out later that Rodney had Jerrica delay all his business commitments so he could spend all his time with me. It was flattering, but then again, my time was running out. Soon, my six-month obligation would end and my debt to Rodney would be paid. I tried not to think about it. I just wanted to enjoy the ride while it lasted.

As the weeks went by, Rodney's kinky scenarios petered out. We spent less time as a dominant bull controlling a submissive sissy and evolved into a more of a couple. We spent more time talking after sex. Rodney became gentler and less demanding. At night, he held me in his arms the same way I used to hold Raegan in my arms. The sex was still amazing, but what bothered me was that this felt natural. It felt like we were having a real relationship.

I was down to my last two weeks. As much as I enjoyed being with Rodney, I was eager to be with Raegan again. I missed her terribly. Fall had been interrupted by an Indian summer. Rodney and I decided to take advantage of the warm weather by hanging out by the pool.

I wore a white bikini and Rodney wore black baggy swim trunks. I did laps while he stretched out on a lounge chair. We had a pitcher of mojitos nearby.

"Hey, beautiful," Rodney said. "Come here. I got something for you."

"Same thing you usually have for me?" I asked as I playfully splashed him.

"Now if you keep that up, I may not give it to you."

"I'm sorry. I'll come and get that something you have for me."

I climbed out of the pool and toweled off. I walked over Rodney's lounge chair and held out my hand. He let me lead him to a chair that he could sit upright in. He began to sit down, but I stopped him. I pulled his swimsuit down to his ankles. He stepped out of them. Though I'd seen it now a hundred times, I still marveled at the sight of his enormous cock and the way it hung between his legs.

As Rodney leaned down to kiss me, I stroked his cock. I could feel it come alive in my hand. I put my hands on his chest and directed him to sit down. I folded my towel, placed it on the ground in front of his feet, and kneeled between his legs.

I licked the drop of pre-come off the tip of his cock and savored the salty sperm. Then I put Rodney in my mouth and bobbed up and down. He leaned back his head and moaned.

His pleasure made me hard. I yanked down my bikini bottom so that I could stroke myself while I sucked on his cock. I reached up and tweaked his nipples and was rewarded with a deep groan. I quickened my pace and slid my mouth up and down his shaft.

"I can't take much more of this," Rodney said. "Climb on this bad boy. I want to fuck that sweet pussy of yours."

I quickly pulled my bikini bottom down and kicked it aside. I had a tube of lube on a side table right next to the sunscreen lotion. I squirted a glob of lube into my hand and smeared it into my ass. I climbed onto his lap, facing him. Rodney guided his cock into my butt pussy. Once I was impaled, he grabbed my ass cheeks. I held onto his shoulders while we fucked like horny badgers.

I came first, sperm erupting out of my bouncing dick and onto his stomach. And then Rodney let out a ferocious growl as he came. I could feel his massive cock jerking inside me.

"Did you like my something?" Rodney said, panting.

"It was really something, that's for sure," I said.

As I kissed Rodney, I heard clapping. We both twisted around to see who was there. Penelope stood on the other side of the pool.

"Bravo," she said. "That was really hot. I'm so glad I caught the show."

I climbed off of Rodney and put my bikini bottom back on. Rodney stood and pulled his swimsuit back on. He glared at Penelope. She smirked and crossed her arms. My face flushed with embarrassment. I was well aware that the people who worked for Rodney knew that he and I were fucking. Hell, they knew that was what I was here for before I knew. So having Penelope catch Rodney and me having sex wasn't a big deal.

What bothered me was that when I first came to the mansion, I had watched Penelope screw a black man with a large cock in the exact same chair and in the exact the same way that I had just screwed a black man with a large cock. I had followed in her footsteps.

"Penelope," Rodney said. "You getting settled in okay? You need anything?"

"An invitation to a threesome would be nice," she purred. "But that probably won't happen. I can see you two lovebirds want to be alone. Hope to see you both around some time."

She turned and disappeared into the house. I poured a glass from the pitcher of mojitos and downed it in one gulp before collapsing into a chair. Rodney sat in a chair next to me and took my hand.

"I'm sorry, Colette," he said. "I should have told you that Penelope was moving back in."

"I'm not upset," I said. "She just caught me off guard. Besides, you didn't have to tell me. This is your house."

"Yes, but it could be…"

"Could be what?"

A dark cloud passed briefly over Rodney's face, but then he smiled.

"Nothing. Hey, we should get cleaned for dinner."

"You're right."

I sensed that these last two weeks were going to be difficult, fraught with conflicting emotions. I didn't know the half of it.

CHAPTER EIGHTEEN
JEALOUSY REARS ITS UGLY HEAD

A week later, I entered my bedroom after my morning workout with Jerrica. I was covered in sweat and looking forward to a good hot shower. I was surprised to find Penelope sitting on my bed. I was always amazed at how stunningly beautiful she was. Her chestnut brown hair flowed down her shoulders. She wore tight ripped jeans and a red halter top. I wondered what she looked like when she was a man. She had to have been extremely handsome.

"Hello Penelope," I said. "Something I can help you with?"

She slithered off the bed and slinked around me.

"I didn't recognize you at first," she said. "You're Cole, the chauffer."

"That was just one of my jobs when I first came to work here."

"I saw you at work in one of the other jobs you do around here. I got the impression from the way you threw yourself into it that you love your work."

She was baiting me, hoping to get a reaction. I was going to disappoint her. I wasn't angry, just curious why she was trying to start something with me.

"It's nice to have you back, Penelope. I'm sure Rodney missed you."

"Did he miss me? Did he ever talk about me while I was gone?"

I walked right into that one. I decided to be honest.

"No. He didn't. But then, he doesn't talk about that kind of stuff with me."

"What do the two of you talk about?"

"Whatever is on our minds."

Penelope opened my closet and rifled through my clothes. She pulled out the red evening gown that Rodney picked out for me to wear to our first romantic date. She held it up to her body. It was too long for her. She tossed it on the floor.

"Do you know why I left?" Penelope said, an edge of anger in her voice. "To make Rodney jealous. To make him see how much he needed me. But instead, he just took the next chauffer and turned him into his sissy bitch the same way he turned me. I never realized how easy I was to replace."

"It's not like that, Penelope. I'm not here to take your place."

"Really, Cole? Because it certainly looks like it."

Penelope whirled through the bedroom, pulling dresses out of the closet, knocking make-up off the vanity table, and pulling panties and bras out of the drawers. In one short burst of manic energy, she had made a huge mess. I was beginning to see why things didn't work out between Penelope and Rodney. The girl was nuts.

What was even crazier than her was how incredibly hot she was. Part of me wanted to rip her clothes off and fucked the shit out of her knowing full well that it would be the ride of my life. The other part of me was scared to death of the bitch.

"It's too complicated to explain," I said, trying to calm her down. "But it's not what you think it is. This is all temporary."

Penelope pulled off her halter top revealing her large perky breasts. Whoever made them did a fabulous job.

"Rodney is like Dr. Frankenstein," she said as she squeezed her breasts. "He's good at creating monsters, but he doesn't know how to deal with them once he breathes life into them."

I moved toward her slowly, afraid that she might take a swing at me. I took her hand and had her sit beside me on the bed. I tried not to stare her tits, but then gave up and stared at them anyway.

"Listen, Penelope. You don't have to worry about me. I'm leaving in a week. That's my deal with Rodney. So I'm not taking your place. I have nothing to do with whatever is going on between you two. I think you need to sit down and tell him how you feel."

Tears fell down her cheeks. I put my arm around her shoulder to comfort her. She used her halter top to dry her eyes. She gave me a weak smile.

"Really?" she said.

"Really. A week from now, I'm out of here."

She looked around the room. "I'm sorry I made a mess of your bedroom."

"That's okay. I'll let the maid clean it up. That's what Rodney is paying her for."

Penelope laughed. She looked down at her bare chest and then cocked her head at me.

"You want to touch them?" she asked.

"You don't mind?" I stammered.

"Not at all. Grab a handful."

I put my hands on her tits. They felt great, almost like the real thing.

"I can give you the name of my doctor in case you ever decide to get a pair of your own."

"It's tempting, but no thank you."

CHAPTER NINETEEN
THE THINGS WE DO FOR LOVE

"You're not going to believe this," I said. "But we're out of lube. Or maybe it's quite believable considering how often we use it."

"We're not out," Rodney said. "There's some in the top drawer."

He pointed at the walnut dresser on the other side of the bedroom. We had been hanging out in his bedroom since dinner, talking and generally just enjoying each other's company. I had already discreetly gone to the bathroom earlier to cleanse my colon.

I was wearing Rodney's favorite lace teddy and he was wearing silk boxers. We weren't in a hurry to have sex. Putting it off created a delicious anticipation that would make the eventual release all the more intense.

I opened the top drawer of the dresser. Next to a new tube of lubricant was a box of condoms and next to the box of condoms was a handgun. I didn't have much experience with guns. This one was big and shiny and looked heavy.

"Boy, you take protection seriously," I said. "You keep a gun next to the condoms."

Rodney chuckled. "Of course, I have condoms. I believe in safe sex."

"I thought only guys with little dicks carried guns."

"No, they carry assault rifles. I have a gun for protection. I've been in certain situations where I was glad I had it."

"Have you ever had to shoot somebody?"

"No and if I'm lucky I never will. But better safe than sorry."

I decided it was time to drop the subject. I took the tube of lube and closed the drawer. I put the tube on the nightstand and got into bed with Rodney. He had his laptop in his lap. He'd been catching up with his emails. Soon I would have to deal with six months' worth of unanswered emails.

"There's something here that I need to show you," Rodney said.

"Is this another fisting video?" I said. "I told that there's no way I'm doing that. Your cock is already as big as a fist."

"No, Colette. This is serious."

I looked at the screen and I got a lump in my throat. It was the video of Rodney and his NBA buddies gang raping me in the showers.

"Why are you showing me this?" I said, fighting back the tears.

"This is the only file that exists of this video. I wanted you to personally see me destroy the file."

He hit the delete button and a warning came up asking if he really wanted to delete the file. He hit yes and the video was gone. Just like that.

"Thank you, Rodney."

"I didn't want you to worry that someday I might try to use it to blackmail you."

"We've come a long way since then. I know you wouldn't."

"I'm sorry for what we did."

"Well, from a bad thing came a good thing, right?"

Rodney pulled me close to him and kissed me. He ran his hands over my body with easy familiarity. He lay on his back and I curled up next to him with my head on his chest and my leg draped over his. I made lazy circles around his nipple with my index finger.

"Penelope came to my room today," I said.

I could feel his body tense at the mention of her name.

"That's interesting," he said. "She also came to see me. What did you two talk about?"

"She thought I was trying to replace her. I told her that simply wasn't true and that my relationship with you was more complicated than that. I suggested that she talk to you about it."

Rodney nodded. "That explains a lot. We talked for a long time. Really cleared the air about things that we'd been avoiding talking about. Penelope thinks she's in love with me, but the only person she truly loves is herself. She likes nice things and I'm just another possession to her."

I ran my hand over his stomach.

"I hope I didn't cause a problem."

"Oh no, girl. You did the right thing. I care deeply for Penelope, but I was never in love with her. She's welcome to live here as long as she wants. She's free to fuck whoever she wants to fuck. Whatever she wants, she just has to ask. But I can't give her my heart. That's just not going to happen."

I reached inside his boxer shorts and rubbed his cock.

"What about your cock?" I asked. "Can she have it?"

"Not tonight."

He pulled off his boxers and I wiggled out of my teddy. We made love slowly to make every moment count. As always, his big black cock touched a deep part of me that drove me insane with lust. Once he was inside me, I couldn't get enough of him. His cock was the best drug in the world.

When Rodney finally rolled off of me, panting and sweaty, I rubbed my belly as I savored the afterglow. I wondered if tonight was the first time I had thought of our coupling as making love and not just fucking. Was that another line I had crossed?

I felt a shiver run down my back.

And then, the door flew open. Penelope entered. She was wearing my red evening gown. She clutched a gun in her hands. Rodney and I scooted back against the bed's headboard. Penelope swung the gun from side to side, pointing the weapon at Rodney and me.

"Penelope!" Rodney said. "What the fuck are you doing?"

"If I can't have you, then nobody will," she cried hysterically.

"You don't want to do this, Penelope," I said.

"Colette's right," Rodney said. "Put the gun down."

"He's already picked out his girl name?" Penelope said. "Stop lying to me, Rodney. You chose him instead of me. You love him instead of me. Admit it, you love him."

With her attention focused on Rodney, I eased out of the bed and inched my way toward her.

"It's true," Rodney said. "I love Colette. I've never been in love with somebody the way I'm in love with her. But I didn't plan to fall in love with her. She was just going to be another stuck up white dude that I turned into a sissy bitch. Then something happened between us. She was different. She made me different."

He held out his hands in a helpless gesture. The man obsessed with controlling others couldn't control his own heart.

"Then it's true," Penelope said.

She stared without blinking at Rodney. I was close to her, but not close enough. I had to get closer.

"Colette didn't replace you," Rodney said. "I was never in love with you. And be honest, Penelope. You've never been in love with me."

Penelope cocked the gun. I couldn't wait any longer. I lunged at her. She turned and fired. I felt like I'd been hit by a brick wall. I tumbled to the floor. I had a burning pain in my shoulder. Penelope stood over me and pointed the gun at my head.

I fought to stay conscious. The floor was wet around me. Out of the corner of my eye, I saw Rodney cross the room with the speed granted to gifted athletes.

"If I get rid of you then he'll have to love me," Penelope said.

A shot rang out. I clinched my eyes shut and waited for the pain. But it didn't come. I opened my eyes. Penelope had a dazed look in her eyes. She dropped the gun. I couldn't see the blood pouring out of her because it matched the red gown she wore. She toppled over like a limp rag doll.

Rodney stood over me and pressed a towel against my shoulder.

"What were you thinking?" he said. "You took a bullet for me."

"You said you loved me," I said. "It was the least I could do."

His lips moved but I couldn't hear what he was saying. And then the room went black.

CHAPTER TWENTY
A GOODBYE GIFT

I woke up in a hospital bed, but I wasn't in a hospital. I was in the chauffer's bedroom. Monica sat in a chair reading a People magazine. She wore nurse's scrubs. Somehow she managed to make the dull green outfit look sexy. She saw that I was awake and checked me over.

"You're a lucky man," she said. "The bullet didn't hit any vital organs. You're going to have a scar, but I think scars are sexy."

"Why are you dressed like a nurse?" I asked.

"Because that's my job. I'm a private nurse. You didn't think I trained sissies for living?"

"How long have I been out?"

"Just two days, but a lot has happened in those two days. Jerrica told me to let her know the minute you woke up. She'll explain what's going on."

Monica called Jerrica. Ten minutes later, she came into the room. She smiled down at me and stroked my hair.

"Damn, Cole. You took a bullet for Rodney. What the fuck were you thinking?"

"Everything happened so fast. I acted on instinct. I am curious. Why am I not in a hospital?"

Monica and Jerrica glanced at each other. Jerrica sat on the edge of the bed.

"You're about to back to your old life," Jerrica said. "We figured you didn't want the world to know about your life here. So we didn't tell the police you were in the room when Rodney shot and killed Penelope in self-defense."

"But certainly the police will figure it out there was another person in the room."

"You watch too much CSI. As far as the police are concerned, an ex-NBA player's crazy ex-girlfriend tried to kill him and he shot her dead. Case closed. The celebrity gossip shows will be talking about Rodney's fatal lovers' quarrel for months and the publicity will probably do him more good than harm."

"So now what?"

"You need a few more days of bedrest," Monica said.

"And then you're free to go," Jerrica said. "Your debt to Rodney has been paid in full. In fact, he feels like you deserve a bonus."

Jerrica took an envelope out of her jacket pocket and handed it to me. Inside was a check made out to Cole Blankenship for one million dollars.

"I can't accept this," I said.

"Rodney knows it's a crude way of saying thank you for saving his life, but he wanted to make it easier for you to get back to your old life after everything he put your through."

I put the check back in the envelope. Conflicting emotions buzzed through me. Monica sat on the other side of the bed.

"You're probably wondering why Rodney didn't give you the check himself," she said. She saw from my expression that was exactly what I was thinking. "He spent every minute he wasn't dealing with the police or the press to sit here by your side. You did something to him that I was beginning to think wasn't possible. You made him drop his guard long enough to really love somebody."

"She's right," Jerrica said. "I've known Rodney for a long time. I've seen him lust after a whole parade of people, but he's always been too afraid of getting hurt to really fall in love. And then your white butt shows up and he's like a lost puppy dog. He's too brokenhearted to face you."

I turned the envelope over in my hands.

"Why doesn't he ask me to stay?"

"Would you stay?"

I bit my lower lip. "No. I wouldn't. I have to go back. Raegan is waiting for me. I gave up too much not to go back to her."

"Well, if you go back to Raegan and then change your mind, let me know. You will always have a room waiting for you here. Damn, Cole, what am I going to do without my workout partner?"

Jerrica threw herself on me and gave me a big hug. It hurt like hell because she squeezed my wounded shoulder, but I didn't care. I was going to miss her too.

She left the room sniffling and rubbing her eyes. Monica checked to make sure she hadn't busted my stitches.

"It will take a couple of months for the hormones to leave your system," Monica said. "So you're still going to look girly for a while."

"That's okay," I said. "If anybody says anything I'll come up with some kind of excuse."

"I can have Jerrica bring in Kenny to give you a boy haircut, though I hate to see you lose this beautiful long hair."

Monica ran her hand through my hair.

"Naw," I said. "I want to keep it long for a while. I can tie it back in a ponytail. I've always wanted to look like an old hippy."

"Or a tomboy."

"God, I'm going to miss you."

Monica got up and smoothed down her scrubs.

"Damn it, Cole. Now you're going to make me cry." She turned to leave, but then faced me again. "Can I ask you a favor?"

"Sure. Anything."

"Until you're ready to leave, can I call you Colette?"

I nodded. "I'd like that."

CHAPTER TWENTY-ONE
THAT DAMNED DRESS

I'd run out of excuses. Despite a twinge of pain when I moved my arm a certain way, my shoulder had healed. I was strong enough to leave on my own steam. I was dressed in the clothes I wore when I first arrived, Oxford shirt, jeans, and sneakers. I had my wallet, keys, and phone in my pockets. I walked out to the front of the mansion. My Lexus was parked in the visitor space behind the fountain. It had a full tank of gas. I had the envelope with the check from Rodney in my back pocket. All I had to do was get into my car and drive home to my wife.

I looked back at the mansion. When I first laid eyes on this place I felt like a minnow about to be swallowed by a whale, but for six months it had been my home. During that time, my life had changed in ways that would probably take me years to sort out.

I put my hand on the door handle of the Lexus. All I had to do was get in and drive home to my wife.

But first, I would call Raegan and let her know I was coming home. I took out my phone and dialed our home phone. It rang and rang. I didn't want to leave a message. I was about to hang up when Raegan answered. Her voice was the sweetest sound in the world.

"Hello?"

"Raegan, it's me, Colette. I mean, Cole."

"Cole! Oh my God. You're finally done."

"Thank you for waiting for me. I was afraid you wouldn't."

"I told you I would. Are you coming home?"

I looked at the mansion. Wasn't I already home?

"When I asked you to wait for me, you said you would unless I told you not to wait for me any longer. Do you remember saying that?"

There was a long silence. I thought maybe my phone had died.

"Yes. I remember."

"Don't wait any longer for me."

"I understand completely. I won't wait any longer. Have a good life, Cole."

I was about to hang up when Raegan called my name.

"What is it, Raegan?"

"Maybe, just maybe, someday, we can be black cock white hungry sluts together. Do you think you could handle that?"

"Would you really want to do that?"

"I think it would be wonderful."

"Let me think about it."

I hung up. I marched back into the mansion and hurried up to my old bedroom. It was quiet as a tomb. I went through the closets until I found it. I knew it would still me in there. There was no way Rodney would throw it out. I was all thumbs with excitement as I put it on. I checked myself out in the mirror. It fit perfectly.

I found Rodney lying in bed. He looked so pitiful sitting in the dark. I flipped on the light switch. He was shocked to see me and even more shocked to see what I was wearing.

I was wearing the French maid's outfit. I had stuffed my bra to make it seem like I had breasts pushing out of the bodice. I had on black fishnet stockings and black spiked heels. The frilly skirt was so short you could see my white lace panties. I had put on a ton of eyeliner and the reddest lipstick I could find. I was a sex fantasy come to life.

"Your maid is here, sir," I said. "How may I serve you?"

Rodney climbed out of bed and faced me. His eyes filled with tears.

"Cole. Does this mean you're staying?"

"The name's Colette. And I was thinking that I would like breast implants. Nothing too big. Just something nice enough for you to play with and to suck on my nipples. But forget about a complete sex change. I like my dick too much."

"So do I."

I was fighting back tears too, but I refused to cry. I didn't want to mess up my mascara. At least, not yet.

"Well, like I said, your maid is here. Your wish is my command."

"My wish is for you to take off that damned dress and never put it on again."

"No," I said firmly. "You take it off me."

Rodney smiled wickedly. "Your wish is my command."

THE END